.Exe Book 2
By Rose Sinclair
& Alexandra Tauber

Copyright © 2015 by Rose Sinclair and Alexandra Tauber
ISBN-13: 978-1-7359375-4-0

ArtOverChaos.com
2021 Edition

People are not a binary.
They are too beautiful,
and destructive for that.

VARIABLE CURRENT

<chapter one>
<! -- Sonia -->

"You meet three types of people in an airport: Travelers, lovers, and lawyers," Scott said. I'd have liked to say we were the lovers in this quip, but after fleeing multiple countries to reach Japan we were definitely the travelers. The lovers were a foreign couple celebrating their honeymoon and making the Japanese people returning home silently uncomfortable. That left the lawyers. Unless any of the other passengers were going to stand up and identify themselves, I was not sure who else he was referring to.

"Remember when you said I was controlling?" Scott added. All of his attention narrowed in on me, when it had been splintered among the array of nervous tics he had picked up on the way here like it was his carry on. "I might have done a thing."

I looked at the queue of people leading to customs, but my eyes fell directly over two Japanese police officers that stood with a woman in a suit. Panic set in fast. When I turned to Scott, he gave me a slight smile. "It's all okay. Just be yourself, and remember whatever happens it's completely your choice."

Baggage claim was in front of us, and I wanted to be there. I've done that before, I knew how it went. Scott kissed me on the cheek before the officers ushered us in separate directions.

I kept looking over my shoulders, expecting them to arrest him, before my escort stopped in a small interview room. Through the glass door I could just see Scott. He was now seated and very still, as if a step removed and frozen as he watched everything.

I hadn't paid much attention to the assumed lawyer but after a glance I knew I'd be able to recall the pattern of her freckles. Her English was very practiced, suggesting she has done international work before and introduced herself as Otsuki.

"What is going on?" I asked.

"You are going to be interviewed about what Mr. Gris had requested."

I met her eyes. "What did he request?"

She blinked, the tiniest hint of being thrown off, and I noticed a small scar like I've seen on others from implants. I knew an answer was about to come, at least that was until an older-looking officer walked into the room. It took everything for me to reign in my emotions, a skill I had once been far too good at. When I looked for Scott again, he was missing.

"Kon'nichiwa, Otsuki-sama," he greeted her before addressing me. "Do you speak Japanese?"

If he knew about HIDs, he knew that answer. I nodded slightly, but he switched to English all the same. "Probably best to interview you in English either way. It is your native tongue, is it not?"

"As far as I know." He smiled, but I wondered if he truly understood or was trying to be personable. "What's going on?"

"We are expediting your naturalization," Otsuki-san said.

I stayed silent, mulling over the words as if I misheard. That, we had not planned for. Or maybe I should say I hadn't.

Coming to Japan was rolling the dice with our fate since being wanted made border-crossing risky. "Your companion has a convincing plea on your behalf. One aided by the fact that Japan has declared the displaced workers from the company formerly known as Ultimate Synthetics as a humanitarian crisis."

My jaw fell open, but he continued on seamlessly. "Let's get started, could you explain that experience?"

I glanced at Otsuki-san, who gave me a firm nod that I was sure was meant to reassure. "I'm glad it's now, as you said, a former company."

"Could you explain what you did as a Human Information Device," the immigration officer said.

"Drive, Ando-san," Otsuki-san corrected with a practiced tone that was purely informative.

He looked down at his paperwork. Expression twitching like he always messed that up. "My apologies."

I cleared my throat. "I transferred information between clients and the company itself."

He nodded for a moment, opening his small folder and removing a few pages and a notepad. "And you worked for multiple contracts, is that right?"

"If one can freely work for a corporation run on human trafficking."

The expression on his face became grim. "Do you feel you're still a victim of those crimes?"

I folded and unfolded my hands in my lap. "There are other victims that may never recover from this. Our plan was only to seek asylum."

"From what?" he asked, his pen coming to a stop.

"From a world that doesn't always see me as a person. From the people that want to continue to use me as a tool, and silence the truth." I paused, the words leaving a bitter taste. "I'm not prepared to convince you I'm worthy of naturalization. Scott... didn't even tell me he was requesting it."

A few papers were pushed towards me. "We received this letter during your flight here. What do you think he means to do by setting this all up?"

I reached out to read over the first page: Months ago, I and some far better activists exposed the truth of UltSyn's human trafficking and rights violations. Whatever judgement is passed on me, I have one request. The same that I had at the start of this whole thing. Protect the workers.

I leaned back in my seat. Too nervous to read any more right now. Where was Scott? Were they nicely asking him questions, or hauling him somewhere far less friendly? "He sent this to you? Today?"

"Mr. Gris sent this to all countries that were considering labeling the displaced workers as refugees since proof of citizenship was causing a problem," Otsuki-san explained. "As far as I know, as his lawyer I'm among the few that knew Japan was your true destination."

My mouth went dry. Did she know about our boat ride to Morocco? Who snuck us out of England? The fear of being stopped any second at the first airport? I flattened my expression nevertheless, and looked at Ando-san. "Scott and I have the same belief that UltSyn committed a crime that cannot be ignored. I don't know where any other HIDs will end up. Some won't have families to find. We were only useful for how well we performed. I held my own in that world, but in this new one?" I touched the letter again, softly curling a finger around the edge of the paper. "We won't be able to do it alone. And I don't want to be done helping those who need me either."

I hadn't expected any words to come out, but each had built on the last until something of value was created. Otsuki-san's slight smile confirmed it. "Is that your goal for your time here?" Ando-san asked. I nodded, feeling utterly speechless now. He slid paperwork towards me. "Citizenship is something that should not be taken lightly. You should have a lawyer present to sign this."

"Miss Larsen," Otsuki-san said, like he had prompted her. "I'd like to officially fill the position if you'd like."

I looked at Otsuki-san, feeling breathless but needing to find words to accept. "Scott reached out to you for a reason, so yes, please."

There was a sudden realization that for the first time I had a choice of being here. Of becoming a citizen and counted as part of a country. Signing these papers were my choice, and the people watching me weren't going to use me for it this time. I skimmed over the papers, but the weight of my choice made it hard to even recall if Japanese citizens had jury duty. And if my mind wasn't tracking, it only meant one thing. I had already made the choice.

I pulled the pen across the paper with a swift movement, and it was done. Well, the first step. In a haze, I listened about how the final papers would come after I found a permanent residence. Which apparently now was the next step to this entirely too new world.

My new lawyer stayed by my side while we walked out to the other side of customs. The suitcase I brought had been searched during the interview so at least that saved a step. I bit down on my lip while looking for Scott again. "Where is he?"

"He must be still getting interviewed. I'd have gone but he told me I should stay with you."

The urge to tell her to just go was strong, but I thought she meant she wasn't allowed to go after the start. I wanted to hold my breath until this whole thing was over and I knew he was safe. I heard my name and hope flared alive in my chest.

Casio jogged towards me and several people turned to watch him. When they started taking photos, my confusion grew. He hugged me before offering to carry my bag. "Scott said you were doing well, but I'm so glad to see you again. We should go somewhere more private while we wait." I opened my mouth to ask what was going on, but his sudden grin interrupted me. "You were on the radio on my drive over. I assume you were on the news as well. But to be fair, being Black has proven itself an oddity of its own here."

I blinked, amazed at... everything. He looked happier than the last time. His hair had puffed out from growth too, which also suited him.

As he got moving, he greeted Otsuki-san in fledgling Japanese before focusing back on me. "I let Terry know you got cleared. I haven't heard from Scott in an hour. Have you?"

I shook my head, too worried for anything else. What if Scott doesn't get released? I closed my eyes trying to mentally shove the idea out of my head. A flash ruined the dark safe place I was trying to imagine.

"I suspect our anonymity has ended," Otsuki-san said.

I opened my eyes to a small collection of reporters with larger cameras than what seemed necessary. They were orderly, but almost nerve-wracking. It was as if we were zoo animals behind glass.

"Can we duck in there?" Casio asked.

I glanced over, not knowing why he'd think I'd know, when more rational minds prevailed.

"Yes." Otsuki-san broke off to talk to an airport worker, who ushered us off into an employee lounge so we could avoid making a scene.

"What do we do now?" I asked.

"We wait."

Casio sighed, and checked his watch of the same name. I almost asked for the time myself. We had rushed, rushed, rushed to get here and my acceptance here was like pulling a band-aid. Quick, and mostly painful in the lead-up.

I don't know how long it took. Forever in compassion for how long it took for me. Casio had checked his watch four times, and I think our lawyer tried to intervene at least twice. The last time she was able to at least relocate us to the part of the airport that Scott was in. When he finally stepped out, I wanted to rush to him like we were in a Hollywood movie.

"Wait here," Otsuki-san said. Fear kept my feet planted. Casio gave me a sympathetic glance, and I think if we were closer, he would have offered another hug.

I watched Scott at an excruciating distance. The humor he managed to find when landing had been lost. When Otsuki-san spoke, he only nodded, shook his head, or gave dreadfully short answers.

A minute later, she waved us over. My hug was more of a collision that caused Scott to step back so we didn't fall. His reaction lagged and I quickly figured out his welcome hadn't been as warm as mine.

"You're home now," he said softly. I knew he meant Japan, but while in his arms it was too easy to pinpoint him as that fabled location.

I pulled back before I made a scene. "You wrote a letter?"

Scott nodded, a bit more freely as time went on. "Yeah, I mistyped too."

Casio took a step closer to greet Scott. His lack of formal reintroduction confirmed they hadn't been out of contact for that long. "I was wondering who was going to get the honor of having you two couch surf."

Scott's eyes flickered over to Casio as his hand stayed nested in mine. There was a spark of mischief there that suggested Scott just needed to mentally reboot. "What can I say? Never bet against me."

Pleased, I turned to ask our lawyer what was next, but she wasn't there. After half a second of panic I noticed that she had excused herself to take a phone call at a polite distance.

"Thanks to your letter, Terry already has a half dozen former UltSyn workers in Hong Kong ready to petition for citizenship," Casio said. "Morocco, however, is under too much scrutiny for their maritime and airspace laws after you came and went through it."

Scott nodded again. The same sort as before that accepted knowledge more than agreeing. When his hand twitched in mine, I decided I should add more to Casio's reports. "That's okay. I don't think they had any stationed HIDs there anyways."

"That's good," Scott said. "I don't want them to be ignored because they had the misfortune of us fleeing through their country. Speaking of, is Roxy in any trouble for getting us to Morocco?"

"She and Naomi made it back to open waters without a hiccup," Casio said. "They mentioned something about a second honeymoon after the stress, but otherwise, all good."

"Mr. Gris." The voice of our lawyer was starting to get familiar, but people calling Scott by his real last name was not. "Your stuff is at the upper baggage claim. You aren't cleared to leave, but you may go pick it up."

"Alright, thank you."

His calm reply almost made me miss a very important comment. The three of them started heading to pick up his backpack, while I was frozen. "You can't leave?" I asked myself softly, and had to catch up to ask again. "Scott, why did you pre-arrange me being able to stay in Japan, and not yourself?"

He paused as Otsuki-san held the door open for us. "Because I didn't know if it was going to work. Any of it. The boat ride, the plane trip, officials accepting you. I'm wanted on ten counts of murder. That's not a burden you should start a new life with."

"Unfair too," Casio added, now just on this side of the door. "Ash killed at least three of those guys."

Scott turned to glare at him. "Not helping," he said, biting down on the words.

Otsuki-san got us back on track. Which would have been welcomed, if it hadn't also ended the conversation I had tried to start.

We had to travel all the way across the airport to reach another baggage claim, which made it even more obvious that they were treating Scott differently. My carry on hadn't gone far. They treated Scott's like a bomb threat.

Along the way we caught the attention of more reporters that had gotten the news that we were here. Scott kept his head down and followed Otsuki-san, who made a path through the waves of reporters. One, however, was different, and I realized how much foreigners did stand out. Not by just appearance, but behavior. He was behind in the pack, but aggressiveness resulted in him outpacing the others.

"What do you have to say about UltSyn?" the reporter asked, his accent clearly American. "Do you think the only reason you aren't jailed yet is because you are straight and white?"

That caught Scott's attention. He looked up, likely giving anyone with a camera their first proper photo. "I'm not straight," Scott said, more annoyed than when with Casio. Both of them paused: Scott in thought, and the fellow American with confusion. "The rest definitely doesn't hurt."

We got moving again as the reporter fell behind. Scott's bag wasn't just sitting on the baggage carousel, and Otsuki-san had to present her client before the airport worker glanced nervously and handed it over.

Scott checked his bag and scuffed. "Great, lost the tablet and the flash drives." It wasn't a crisis since there were backups on anything on UltSyn that hadn't been leaked already. "If I'm going to be stuck here, we might as well find somewhere nondescript. Hopefully with an outlet."

"Agreed," I chimed in. Mostly because I wanted to circle around to the pressing topic.

"And Wi-Fi," Casio added.

Otsuki-san led us to a lounge area that had a hefty yen price per person to go in. A few quick words with the wide-eyed attendant got us a private room, too. That way, the reporters couldn't just figure it out and pay to get in.

I sat quietly on a sofa wondering if Otsuki-san had been chosen for her ease under pressure. It was something I lacked right now since all of this was more happening to me, rather than with. But maybe she was chosen because of the possible implant I saw.

Scott sat on the floor since his phone cord wouldn't reach far enough to the chair. I figured he was talking to Terry, who had served as our digital guardian angel on the way here. The mounted TV in the corner cut to a live feed, featuring us, which was strange to watch in real time. Thankfully it didn't have our image, just that we were confirmed to be in Japan.

Scott seemed settled. At least that was what I thought, until he kept glancing at a vending machine that held midrange-priced electronics. Chargers, powerpacks, and the like.

"What are you doing?" I asked.

Nothing, he signed distractedly.

"Scott."

"I told you. Nothing. Definitely not learning how to mod the kiosk to give people free tech," he said. "Not like I'm annoyed with mine being taken." Otsuki-san had been ignoring us, but paled as she overheard. "I said definitely not that."

"My man," Casio said, as if he was going to be the voice of reason. "Will your brand of activism ever not be selfless in a selfish way?"

Scott shrugged and worked on his phone for a few lines of code at least. "You both should leave. Before some UltSyn rep decides to charge you as well."

"Do you really think they are going to charge me with trespassing and a count of cybercrime?" Casio asked.

"A count," Scott mocked without looking up. "And actually, yes. I'm also surprised they haven't charged me with kidnapping."

"They can't do that, right?" I asked Otsuki-san. Her ruling was the one that mattered to me here.

"Not unless you charge him with it," she said.

I exhaled in relief. Thankful again that I couldn't be made into UltSyn's pawn even after their financial demise.

Two hours later we still silently and stubbornly waited with Scott. "Do you think PrlC is price control?" he asked.

I rolled my eyes as Casio got up and went to crouch down beside him. Otsuki-san's phone rang, and I wanted to eavesdrop on that discussion instead, but she had excused herself again. After minutes of studying the code, Casio agreed. "How are you going to make changes though?"

Scott glanced to see if Otsuki-san was watching before answering. "Spoofing the price matching."

"That's clever. I would have tried the admin diagnostics route," Casio said. "Could I score some better headphones right now?"

"You'll have to come back in a few days to test it," Scott replied, but quickly grew hushed as Otsuki-san came back.

"The word is that the Japanese immigration service is waiting to see if the United Kingdom files further paperwork," she explained. "Since your passport was valid when you landed you were automatically granted a 90-day tourist visa."

"Does that mean Japan has three months to decide if Scott can stay?"

"*Hai.* It's unlikely anyone in this country will rule either way until we know the UK's next move. Which could be hours or weeks of back and forth since there is no extradition treaty. Earlier, I got a ruling and by a Russian precedent, your 90 days doesn't start until you leave the airport. But we should be careful to avoid seeming overeager in regard to further traveling."

"So, this is my purgatory," Scott stared out towards the bland colored walls and over the teal green carpet with an odd x shape in shades of blue and bits of red. I thought he might lean his head back, look up to a god I never saw him pray to. But pain so often comes from not knowing. To close his eyes would have been the acceptance stage of grief, and I'm pretty sure Robin Hood-style hacking counted as the frustration phase.

Casio got up to try, and after simply telling the machine what he wanted, scored himself those new headphones. Scott followed as if to study his handiwork. While Casio seemed tickled, Scott frowned. "I must have messed up the countdown code."

Scott returned to sit by himself on the floor. It was clear he wasn't replacing his lost stuff, just trying to keep busy.

After fleeing, doing nothing felt like running on empty. Fear of getting caught had actually made everything go by fast. This tension from waiting was worse. If Scott were taken from me now it would been too calm, and without a fight.

I moved close, and considered leaning my head against his shoulder, but opted instead to just lay down and put my head on his lap. He wordlessly adjusted to let me. I stared up at him for a moment before shutting my eyes.

"My phone should be charged, so I can move to the couch if you really want," he asked, but if he needed the distraction, I didn't want to take it from him.

Between drifting off and fighting off trying to guess the probability we'd have to go into real hiding, I felt his finger ever so gently run though my hair. It was enough that I felt safe even with the uncertainty looming.

Next thing I knew, I woke up to Scott talking to Casio as he crouched close by. "Casio's going home for the night," Scott said to me. "You should call it a night too."

I sat up too fast and the blood rushed to my head. "I won't go."

"You can rest. Comfortably. Maybe eat something more than junk food," Scott said. "You don't need to be here for this."

"I'll be here as long as you're here."

"Sonia…"

"Stop asking." I knew he felt like I was stuck because of him, but I didn't want to be anywhere else. "I made up my mind. I'm going to get a coffee as I walk Casio out."

He glanced at the both of us, before wishing Scott good night. We paused before reaching the doors that led outside. "You must know he's pushing you away so you are safe. No one knows what's going to happen, and all of us have been trying to get you both out of London since that night."

I nodded while looking at the ground. That was when he kept me close for my safety. After nearly being fried by UltSyn's mainframe, I'd had no idea which direction was up for a while. "It's not really going to be freedom without him."

Casio nodded, and pulled up a smile. "Good night, Sonia. Call me the second you need that place to crash."

"We will." I waved goodbye, and had to settle for really shit coffee on the way back since everywhere that served anything good was now closed. I thought about grabbing Scott a cup, but it was an undue punishment.

When I returned, Scott was standing next to Otsuki-san. He was pinching the bridge of his nose and was desperately trying not to say whatever he was thinking.

"What's wrong?" I asked.

"Nothing," Scott said, like a repeating record. "I'm going to go to the bathroom."

It was one of those moments where I felt like I should follow, but felt too awkward.

"Does he do that often?" Otsuki-san asked.

"Do what?"

"Hold his tongue."

I glanced at where Scott had left. He was out of sight, but thankfully the private lounge meant he wasn't far. "No, actually."

Otsuki-san's light sound of consideration caught my attention. "It's a trait that will help him here."

I wanted to take solace in that, or that any minute now we could get good news about leaving, but a new problem quickly appeared. Scott hadn't returned. I'm never sure at what point you are allowed to follow someone into a bathroom; I think at some point you just get too worried and just do it.

"Scott?" I called. I didn't think anyone else was in here, and doubted I could play a foreigner clueless enough to confuse the bathrooms if they were. When he didn't answer I went in. There was an electronic sign by the door that showed what stalls were taken. But none said they were occupied. "Where are you?"

I rounded a corner to where the sinks were and found only Scott. He was leaning over on his hands, avoiding the mirrors with the low hang of his head. My steps quickened before stopping short to analyze everything. His hands were balled with white knuckles, veins tracing along his arms as his body strained with tension. When I moved around the side, I noticed his jaw was locked and his eyes were tightly closed.

"Scott, I... don't know how to help. But please, tell me what's going on in there and I can try."

There was utter silence, and then softly, "What will you do if I get extradited?"

"That's not—"

"You know it's a possibility, so please don't... try to make it better." He looked over at me. "What will you do?"

"I'd follow you."

"To jail? No, you'd lose everything. And everything is so—" Even if I had wanted to cut him off, I didn't need to. His words were interrupted by a harsh breath through gritted teeth, and I watched the tension release into a tremble.

"Oh, hon." I felt no other choice than to reach out and touch his hand. He flinched before the weight of my hand steadied it. "I'm here. And I'm not going anywhere."

"What if I don't belong here?" he asked. "Everything is so different. The language is different, fuck, even these toilets." His breathing was betraying him, as if he were running out of air. "I'm out of my depth."

"You'll figure it out."

"I don't even know if I deserve to try," Scott added, quick enough that I didn't think he was listening to me. "I wasn't given a second chance, I took it."

Scott's eyes flickered up to me as unshed tears brought out their color in a way that I felt should be triumphant. But it wasn't.

"I killed people." His words were all too serious for this place. I had almost expected them to echo, as defeat haunted his soul. "Is this justice?"

I didn't know how to answer that question, because I knew Scott wouldn't be the type to let me bullshit him. 'It's okay' or 'You did your best' simply would not cut it. I pressed my lips together, thinking of a proper answer, and when I feared Scott might take my silence for a no, I spoke. "Have you heard of the Trolley Problem?"

"The thought experiment?"

"Yeah. There is a runaway trolley barreling down the railway tracks," I explained in an effort to distract him from his own thoughts. "Five people are tied on the tracks and a trolley barrels towards them. You find yourself in the train yard, next to a lever that can save them. But touching the lever means the person standing on the side track will be killed instead."

"The Trolley Problem has no answer." He pulled himself to sit on the counter, like he had resigned himself to live in this non-western restroom. "Hasn't it been debated since like, what, the 1950s?"

I nodded. "In every way, from every angle."

Helpful.

I loved when he sarcastically signed. One could read every bit of the word from the brush of his hand off his chin to his hands tapping against the other to finish.

"I don't have an answer for you," I said, and moved closer. "Because there is no 'right' answer. It's unanswerable. I also believe that your intent was good, and your impact was good for good people."

"Maybe you are biased," he whispered.

"Maybe." I could concede that much. "I could cite an increase of participants who find that saving five at the cost of one is morally unethical as long as the one was a loved one."

"Really?"

"There's a 25.2% increase in believing that it's wrong in that situation. You risked your own life for your sister. For me. And all the others, too. To make the question a fair comparison, one would have to ask if it is ethical to save the one, at the cost of the five, if you knew an unknown number would be hurt if you didn't."

Scott rubbed a hand over his mouth and chin. In this harsh light, you could see hadn't shaved. "I guess that's what they are debating now."

"Yeah." I placed my hand on his cheek to lift his eyes to meet mine. Instead of some grandiose gesture or distraction, I leaned my forehead against his. "And we will learn their answer together. I know mine."

With our eyes closed I could hear Scott's hands tighten on the counter by the slight catch of his nails. He exhaled sharply, and I assumed it left him mostly tired instead of in a hazed panic.

"Will you come back out now?" I asked softly.

"Yeah," he said, "just give me a minute."

I glanced around to grab him paper towels, but I didn't even see hand dryers. This bathroom was just different enough to be unnerving. I could speak the language, but that didn't mean I understood Japan better than an English-to-Japanese dictionary. This however, was not a confession to be made right now when he was feeling cultural shock. "I'll wait for you outside."

Sleeping in an airport wasn't the worst place I'd ever slept. I didn't expect Scott to get any sleep due to a mixture of stress and stubbornness, but when I woke up, he was leaning against me with his eyes closed. I made a silent vow to move as little as possible.

This plan of course did not last long, since I had been woken up by Otsuki-san's phone and, two buzzes later, so was Scott. It was a slow day. If I could have removed it from our histories nothing would have changed. We sat being equally as worried that the news cycle had moved on as we were reassured by it.

The next day, Otsuki-san's presence was again the only noteworthy thing in our morning, this time in a completely different way. She had stepped back into the room and stopped as she stared down at her left leg. Her hand reached down to her knee as if she had twisted it on her walk back.

I thought nothing of it besides a tinge of sympathy, but Scott got up. "May I help you?" Otsuki-san looked up at him and nodded. He helped her over to a seat and I got up, worried she was hurt.

"What is it doing?" Scott asked, softly as he sat on the edge of the seat next to her.

"Just freezing up. I'm hoping the signal will sync back up soon." Her English was less fluid, not that I blamed her in the slightest. Last time I was really stressed, I couldn't even get a proper sentence out.

"My friend told me that the shielding accidently blocks the frequency. If you trust me, I could try to fix it for you," Scott said.

The airport around us was moving at normal speed, but in our little room, time froze. I know she had taken our case, not just mine, but for the first time I wondered if she did trust Scott. Believing your client just wasn't necessary for representing them.

"Could you lift your slacks up?" Scott added.

I don't think what was going on fully clicked until Otsuki-san pulled her pant leg up. A prosthesis attached just above the knee, or at least the cut of her slacks made it appear that way. The scar I thought was for implants of the same vein as mine had a very different purpose.

Bashfulness might have been expected from having a person you hardly knew delicately touching you, but Scott was so focused on the tech that it seemed to save her from any obvious embarrassment. He talked her through exactly what he was doing, even if he was just looking for what to do.

I watched what could only be described as a surgery of sorts as Scott kneeled in front of her prosthesis, with a small hatch open that allowed access to the motherboard.

"Here we go," Scott said. His hand blocked what he was doing, and a moment later he held up a tiny piece of metal. "Give that a try."

Otsuki-san wiggled her ankle, before moving her leg as a whole. "Thank you. That does feel more responsive. What was that part meant to do?"

Scott stood and held out his hand again for her to test it further. "It's meant to act as a late addition heatsink, but this is a far cry from one."

"May I see?" I asked as Otsuki-san had moved on to a slight bounce before giving walking a go. Scott handed it over, and the sliver of metal sat in the palm of my hand. Funny how our best engineering can be foiled by, well, a foil.

"Please let me know if it heats up on you," Scott added with a growing smile as Otsuki paced back to us. "I'm sure with actual tools I'd be able to help more."

"Thank you. You've helped a lot already."

"That's what he does," I said proudly.

Scott chuckled to himself as he moved back to where he had been. "You don't need to oversell it. I just remembered a flaw in a common system." It didn't seem to be the time or place to boast, but he saw someone with a problem and worked out a solution. Methods could be debated, but it was what Scott always did.

The call we had been praying for came with less than an hour left in the work week, and with the threat of spending the weekend here hanging over our heads. I can't even remember if Otsuki-san had tried to step away to take it, and we had simply been drawn back towards her knowing this would be it.

She hung up and turned towards us, and I tried not to read into her neutral expression. "No more paperwork is coming with everyone focused on UltSyn's growing crimes rather than the ones you're accused of," Otsuki-san said. "Parliament isn't risking going after you right now when even their own actions are in question." Scott fell into the nearest seat as I stared breathlessly until she finished. "You are officially sanctioned to be anywhere in Japan for the next 90 days."

"Holy shit," Scott breathed out.

That caught both of our attention, in likely different ways. I gave Otsuki-san a reassuring look before going to Scott.

"This is real, right?" he asked, eyes wide. "It's not just aggressive wishful thinking?"

"This is happening. We get to stay."

"Holy shit," he repeated.

"Congratulations, Mr. Gris." Otsuki-san said, trying to be a part of our moment even though she didn't seem 100% sure what to make of Scott yet. I could understand that. It had taken me a while originally, too.

"There's no need to be so formal with me," he said. "I owe you my life. Just Scott works."

She seemed to consider this. Maybe comparing what she knew of Americans and what she assumed he knew of Japanese culture. "I'll get working on securing you a more permanent visa, but otherwise are you ready to leave, Scott-san?"

If I was any more excited, I was going to have to answer for him. Scott took a steady breath, my hand, and then stood. "Hai, *arigato gozaimasu*, Otsuki-sama," he said.

I thought when we stepped outside for the first time I'd be filled with a sense of amazement. That I'd be surprised by the sun's bright brilliance or the city's own dazzle. But it was otherwise a plain day even down to statistically average weather. But I think that's what gave me the most hope. Proof that a normal day in an unknown world could be the most beautiful thing ever.

<chapter two>
<! -- Scott -->

Shouganai could fuck off. I think what pissed me off the most about the phrase was how right it was. It's a common phrase here that translates to it can't be helped. I must have heard it at least twenty times already, even Casio said it.

He's the only one who said it directly to me, so maybe my annoyance was coming from others saying it. Just accepting there was nothing to be done while I wanted to help. I, a person who could only talk to people who knew English, or one of several programming languages. In my head *shouganai* sounded like, *You've made your bed, now lie in it.*

Far more guilty, far more *me*, really.

Lying down in my bed was actually exactly what I wanted to do. Except my bed was in a country I wasn't allowed to set foot in. Bed options now included stealing Casio's, stealing the couch (which was now Sonia's), or the floor.

My sigh had enough of an audible exhale that Casio paused with extra throw pillows stuffed under his arms. "Are you okay?"

"I'm fine." I was also a liar. The truth was I was narrowly avoiding further panic attacks from living in a consistent state of fear. I missed London; I was never afraid there. I was actually alarmingly cool with even big things, like getting shot.

Okay, so I could admit my perspective was off. Ask me to break a law in a tech-savvy way, and I'd be your guy. But if you were looking for someone who could calmly take on the adventure of a new and unknown life, well, you'd have to ask someone else.

"Here," Casio said. He handed the pillows over without commentary on my silent on-going freaking out.

"Can I ask you something?" I tossed the pillows on the couch, since even if they were for me, having them on the floor would result in being stepped on. "How do you do it?"

Casio's expression tightened in a way I normally only see when he's confused with a bit of code. "Live in Japan after everything?" When I didn't disagree, he went on. "You find something to do. Get a job, pester Terry for something that feels meaningful when you can afford it. Pick friends up at the airport."

I smiled despite myself. "You aren't planning on needing that favor returned anytime, right? I think I had my fill of airports for a while."

"Nah," Casio playfully dragged out the word. "Might go to the park later though. Got any plans today?"

"Staying off everyone's radar." I pulled out my phone and checked the messages. They were in a spot I still hadn't gotten used to since HALIE, my personally programmed OS, wasn't running on this burner phone. This is why you shouldn't name your electronics. You feel a sense of loss when they are gone. Or in this case after deleting them so they aren't legally used against you.

"I should work on my Japanese," I added. Which made my to do list: Learn Japanese. Get a job. Be a productive member of society. Whatever that means here, if that's even is culturally relevant. Maybe not even in that order.

"Does America do that 'immigrants should learn English' thing, too?" Casio asked. "I used to hear it all the time growing up."

"Oh yeah. That's not just a U.S. thing?"

"Ha, no," Casio answered as he walked across the room. "I think it's a white people thing."

I wasn't going to disagree, but before I could answer anything, Casio handed over a key. "I gave Sonia hers before she ran to the corner store."

"Thanks," I mumbled and placed the key in my pocket, so I could go on pretending not to think about it. But I would. The metaphorical weight of having an ordinary key meant I had to do other ordinary things.

I spent an hour trying to learn new words before Sonia came back. I told myself that, after we put away the small assortment of groceries, I'd work on it more, but I didn't. It was painful to do nothing, and tiresome to adjust to a life that might have a countdown.

Whether it was a sense of boredom or paranoia that brought me to the following suggestion, I'll never know. Or care, to be honest. Everyone was settled, Sonia with a book and Casio in his room. The door was open as he sat at a small desk, so I went straight in. "I've noticed this place is under-fortified compared to what I came to expect with Terry's place. Do you want help with that?"

"Yeah, actually."

I grinned.

"I got a box of spare junk that maybe we can repurpose. Do you want to mess with it tonight?"

"Absolutely."

Casio glanced back at the laptop screen, debating what he was doing with what he could be doing. In the end, he closed the laptop. "Let's see what old toys I have around."

He had a small closet stuffed with banker boxes full of stuff. It was nowhere near as much of a collection of what we both once had access to, but this was a solid collection all the same.

We each took a box from the top and sat on the floor making small piles of cords, peripherals, and just otherwise interesting things. The most interesting find was actually a business card. I wouldn't have given it a second's thought if it didn't have a cell battery built in. I flipped it over to find two small metal plates to place my thumbs. A small old-school display lit up when I completed the circuit, displaying a readout of my heart rate. "Holy shit, it's a tiny EKG."

"Isn't it the coolest? I got it at a medical convention and couldn't toss it."

"I want to see," Sonia said, and I handed it up to her on the couch. She carefully placed one thumb then the other watching it with a stoic expression before offering it back to me. "*Chiisana* EKG."

I stared at her for an unmoving second. "Ti... tiny?"

"Yes." She smiled as I took it back to pass on to Casio, since it was his turn to play with it.

"I wonder how accurate it is," he said and tried to make it mess up or display something different as well as he could without breaking into exercise. "Shame we can't use the little guy for anything."

"Don't you want to protect your place from undead robbers?" Sonia teased.

"Low on my worry list." He chuckled before placing it on the table and getting back to looking for relevant parts. "Oh! Here we go. Terry had a bunch of these for some... thing or another. I forget why he needed them, but I didn't want to trash them."

Casio started to pull apart a small white sticker and I leaned over to see several boxes of what must be RFID chips. "If we put the chip on our keys it's not going to be that safe. How about we rig it so it's like a lock? That way if the tag moves away from the reader, that alerts the system?"

"That gets my vote," Sonia said, "because as much as I like you, Casio, chipping my hand to pay you a visit is taking this to a level I'm not ready for."

I glanced over my shoulder, unsure if she was being dreadful or playful. I still didn't figure it out before Casio got up.

"That's good because I don't have one of those chipping devices anyways." His words became muffled as he went into his bedroom again. "I do have an RFID writer however."

I decided to ignore them both and start looking for a webcam that I was sure was hidden somewhere in the closet, since an alarm wasn't much good if you didn't have a photo of who broke in. "We are going to need a safe word and that washi tape," I said, as I shook a pile of cords to find an end so I could untangle them.

"If you were anyone else," Casio said, "that would be an incredibly weird thing to walk back into."

I turned to find Casio had paused at the foot of his door frame having returned with the reader/writer. "For the webcam, and to install the chips without damaging the walls."

"Webcam?"

I shook the camera free of the nest of cords to show him.

"Ahh, that went with an old gaming system."

"Are you attached to it?" I asked a little rougher than I meant, considering I was lamenting my own tech only a few hours ago.

"No, it's fine. It's built to track movements anyways and will save us a lot of time reprogramming it."

"If it's motion based," Sonia said, completely giving up the sham that she was trying to read from the couch, "you should use sign language instead of a word, it's less obvious. Easier to control if in a crisis situation."

"That." I said pointing to Sonia. "That's clever. We should do that."

We worked on it into the night, and before we all fell asleep, we had programmed in signs for hello, goodbye, emergency, and pizza. The last one would probably have to change since pizza isn't a common meal in Japan, and the idea was completely born out of our being hungry. But it's a neat trick to be able to sign the word for pizza and for it magically to appear at your doorstep. They run small here, so for science we ordered three separate times and surely scored the confusion of the delivery crew.

Working with an agency was new and unusual. I kept expecting to somehow be put on hold even as I walked up to the building. I looped the straps of a surgical mask over my ears and adjusted it across my mouth. It would have been so strange anywhere else, but here it granted me a drop of anonymity.

I handed my pass over to the man at the first desk. Its legitimacy made me more nervous than any of my faked credentials ever had. My exhale was shaky, but stayed hidden as the badge was passed back and I was buzzed into the building.

I paused just inside to stare at the logo of the anti-virus company. The Japanese name was familiar, since their software was international. If I had grabbed a coffee beforehand this morning it would have been objectively perfect, but I had been afraid my stomach would betray me.

The hall was empty since it was before any workers had settled in or interns buzzed around. If I wanted to keep that advantage, I'd have to move fast. This wasn't UltSyn, but it could define me all the same. I headed towards the back, having memorized the layout of this building.

I stopped at every desk and plugged in a key logger at each computer, like Santa went around bringing gifts. I planted six before more workers came in. I ducked into a cubicle and sat in an office chair whose owner wouldn't be back from vacation for another week. Gotta love people oversharing online with a job like this.

As I waited for everyone to sit down, I glanced at the desk, which didn't seem particularly interesting at first. Then I noticed something tucked by the computer. I picked it up to find a little Tron bike. When I flipped it over a USB unfolded from underneath. It took almost everything in me to keep my mouth shut. I didn't know where you could buy these, but they were much cooler than the flash drives I had.

As it turns out, early birds literally do get the worm, and my phone vibrated after receiving their login information. I waited until enough people logged in to feel secure that almost everyone coming in today was seated, before heading for the back door.

A woman making some tea spotted me. I don't know exactly what her words were but I can assume it was something similar to *hey that guy doesn't usually work here.*

I ignored whatever comment it was and moved faster, making it outside and passing a camera that was watching the back exit. Scans of the area didn't reveal it from the street, which only left my options limited. Like climbing over a back way to reach said street and hope my ID couldn't be made.

"Keyloggers are such uninspired hacking, Mr. Gris."

I turned slowly towards the new voice, hands raising to my head. It was more of a habit born from being shot than actual threat of violence, given Japan's gun laws. I tilted my head at the comment, wondering if his translation ended up overly harsh or if he also wasn't impressed with my run of the mill-looking flash drives. "How many did you find?"

"Six." The man reached into his suit pocket to retrieve one of the drives. Several other workers were packed around the door to watch. "This was the best the notorious Hello World Hacker could do? It took all of a minute to figure out what the code did."

"The keylogger was meant to be found, so ask yourself, was that all?" There was so little protection between me and what was going on that I was again thankful for the tiny protective mask. I was unarmed, caught, and shaky with the fear of being branded a criminal in yet another country.

"Please explain."

"Take a look at your software's newest update."

There was the shuffling of people and stray Japanese words here and there as I held deadly still.

"Our antivirus wouldn't be able to find the virus because it is the virus," a worker at the door said. He held up a tablet to show what he meant. "Our program never checks its own code for flaws since updates come approved from us."

"Sure, you caught me when you knew I was coming at some point and paid for me to do so, but you wouldn't have caught the DDOS sequence before it updated worldwide, making every user of your software an unknowing member against the target of my choosing."

The man's face tightened. If he was anywhere else, or anyone else besides the boss, he likely would have cussed. Finally, he laughed. "In this hypothetical situation, you'd risk jail to take down a website?"

"Depends on the website." I smiled, but realized my expression was pointless. "If you threaten a symbol, you can threaten a way of life. Or a reputation, or stock prices. Which to some is the same thing."

The man took a step closer and I did my best not to twitch. I felt my muscles tense reflexively from days where hacking wasn't my job, but a mission that I had literally bled for.

When he offered his hand out, I had to shake my head to reboot my thoughts so I could give my hand in return. Confusion must have been reflected in my eyes.

"Has shaking hands fallen out of practice?" he asked, more curious than offended.

"It's my fault. I'm trying to get used to a Japanese way of doing things."

"We are lucky to have you."

I wasn't sure if he meant Japan was the lucky one or his anti-virus company. Instead of asking, I just bowed. *"Arigatō gozaimasu."*

"Enjoy the rest of your day, Mr. Gris. We need to quickly fix this, and find out why a zero-day vulnerability has survived for so long." His tone grew a bit more annoyed, but I realized it was directed at someone else now.

Definitely the best perk of working freelance was that you got to leave before blame was dished out. My least favorite part was having to figure out the metro with my still piss-poor Japanese skills.

"Honey, I'm home." I signed a hello to the operating system that Casio and I had named Ada on my way in, then pulled off the mask.

"Why, Scott," Casio said, from a barstool at the kitchenette. He took a bite of lunch and I could see his eager amusement. "I'm flattered."

I grinned in lieu of any jest in return. "Where's Sonia?"

"She went to the corner store to get some coffee."

I fell into the couch, eyes closing before even my muscles had a chance to relax. "God, I love that one."

"Tea's just not good enough for some Americans. I get it."

I wasn't sure if he did, so I leaned back and looked over at him. He was no longer facing me and occasionally his hand flipped the page of a magazine. "Despite the lack of pet names for each other, thank you again for letting us stay here. After today's job, we should be able to get out of your hair."

Casio swiveled his chair around. "For the last time, it's not a problem. Here." He reached a hand back over and tossed the magazine onto the couch. "Distract yourself. I don't like to get all touchy-feely before noon."

I leaned forward to grab it and flipped through a few pages. "It's all in Japanese. Wait, I got this." I dug out my phone and opened a translation app. I couldn't even get through the whole page. Hiragana does not translate quickly. "This program needs an update."

Casio picked up his meal as if my commentary were too distracting. I expected him to venture off into the bedroom, but instead I watched as he sat down. "Now improving other people's code is something I'm always game for."

<chapter four>
<! -- Scott -->

I traded in my notoriety like an arcade-goer traded in tickets for candy. It didn't seem to matter that I was being portrayed as a controversial figure in the news. Good or bad, companies simply didn't want to be brought down like UltSyn and decided to pay for my skills instead of suffering them.

The biggest point of contention was actually the question of who suffered the worst? The stock owners, the workers, the people who had contracts with UltSyn, or the families of those involved? I considered myself part of that last group more than anything else, but international coverage seemed to keep forgetting even that.

Victim or devil, being on the news was good for business. I took every freelance job offered in fear that lack of momentum would be the death of me. Otsuki suggested avoiding making any political statements or interviews on related matters at least until Japanese officials decided what type of visa was relevant. That is if I deserved one at all. I could dot my i's and code my t's on demand if that's what it took.

Ada had also come a long way in two months' time. Like the woman herself, the code was a mixture of scientific poetry and dedication. With Casio's help and many overnighters, the new OS was something I think the namesake would be proud of.

This strange combination of infamy, praise, and time afforded us a house. Osaka in no way was a small city, but it was a third of the size of Tokyo. The differences between Casio's downtown apartment there and our house here weren't even on the same scale. He let me take some spare parts which made our possessions a box full of tech, some clothes, and two backpacks. I hoped the accidental minimalism could be fixed, or embraced, since our house was a one-bedroom, one-tatami room anyways.

"Shoes," Sonia reminded me when I was about to take a step in.

"Oh." I pulled off my shoes and left them before the step up. Since this was our house, I could ignore any social norm I wanted, but it would be a good habit to get into.

The first floor was open from the living room to kitchen to bathroom. The only thing that broke up the space was a flower box that extended out eight inches or so in over the kitchen sink's window.

"This is definitely my favorite place we looked at," Sonia said, taking everything in again. The remodel that had been done last year brought in a modern feel that we were both more used too.

"I just hope we can keep it."

"Maybe a housewarming gift will make you feel better. Go wait by the counter or something. I don't want you to peek."

I puffed out my cheeks and did as asked. Our dishwasher was a small domed countertop appliance that looked like a 1990's vision of the future. There hadn't been a day yet without something small being different. With my back turned towards her, I pulled myself up onto the counter.

Sonia dug around for a moment then came over with a gift bag. "For you."

My eyes locked on hers even though they didn't meet mine. "Why didn't you tell me we were doing this?"

Sonia pulled herself up next to me, and swung her legs freely. Her delayed reply made me wonder if we'd ever really belong here.

"How can I explain," she said with a deep exhale. "I don't remember having a traditional home, so this place is literally everything I could ever want. And it's not that I don't love it, but I won't be comparing it to things I've lost like you may."

My mouth opened to object. To remind her that it wasn't a sure thing that I could stay. But I wanted this precious moment with her more, so I said nothing.

"Here," she said, and set the bag, shining a solid metallic blue, in my lap.

I popped open the tape holding it closed and pulled out a white army hat. "I feel like this is joke-gift adjacent," I said, and put it on. "But it fits."

"This is you now," Sonia smiled. "A white hat, who gets legally paid to break into things."

"I love it." I leaned in to kiss her. "Thank you."

"Welcome." Sonia hopped down then wrapped her arms around my neck. "We are homeowners now. What's the first thing you want to do?"

"I am taking us to bed," I said, gesturing to her to take a step back so I could stand myself. When I picked Sonia up she helped by wrapping her legs around my waist. "I'm thinking about sleeping for a solid week."

Sonia laughed softly as I walked us toward the bedroom. "Don't forget that Terry and Nic are coming Thursday."

"Then I'm going to sleep until Thursday."

I carried Sonia upstairs, vowing to get a one level place next time. To the left was the tatami, and on the right, a bed. I set her down next to the low platform that extended past our mattress.

It felt impossibly low on the ground, but I wouldn't had gotten back up for the world. There weren't even sheets on the bed yet, just pillows thrown up near the top from the first time we stopped in after getting the keys.

"You can take the hat off, silly." Sonia bopped the brim with a finger before laying her head on my chest.

"It's better this way, since all I have to do is tilt it to make up for the fact that we don't have drapes." I adjusted the hat so it blocked out light from the window and the veranda's sliding door.

The weight on my chest lifted as Sonia sat up. "It's the gift that keeps on giving."

A mumbled agreement was all I could muster, since the comforting heaviness of sleep weighed down my reply.

When I woke up, I was in London, and my sister was missing. That's what my thoughts screamed as I stared at a blank wall. That was the past. Tori was at home, safe with our parents. Sonia was safe too. I didn't fully believe my reminders until I found Sonia in the kitchen. This happened yesterday too, but never at Casio's, and I didn't get why.

"I'm sorry," Sonia said, as she prepared something over the stove. "Did I wake you?"

"What are you making?" I picked up a cloth napkin with a tight geometric pattern off the table. When did we even get these?

"Scrambled eggs."

"Scrambled eggs?" The napkin's pattern threatened to give me a headache so I dropped it along with my disbelief. "No fish for breakfast today, I take it."

"I was trying to be in the spirit of things yesterday. Would you like some or do would you rather stay grumpy this morning?"

"Eggs please." Instead of being the aforementioned grump, I got up to help make toast.

I'd like to say the day got better from there, but traveling was rocky. Driving to Tokyo was my first thought, but neither of us were licensed, for one. The rail was then the logical choice, being faster and cheaper, but I hated it. Not only wildly overcrowded, but also my pass read "Temporary Visitor" in English, as if to further taunt my anxiety out into the open. Still, hours of travel later, I could at least focus on finding Nic and Terry.

The dining area was boxed in with square panels of colored glass while the name of the place hung overhead like a chandelier that read: SO TIRED. I don't know when or why some words were in English and others not, but whatever the reason it was weirdly endearing here. Not because I thought Japan would tailor itself to me, but that I could to it.

"Scott."

I glanced around, stopping when my eyes fell on Sonia. She tilted her head towards our friends, whom I now spotted sitting on the patio on the other side of the stained glass.

Terry stood when he saw us, and Nic stayed sitting with a smile on his face. I wasn't sure if Terry was going to go with a handshake or hug; neither option would have surprised me. What was noteworthy, however, was the muscle he had picked up.

"I swear this isn't a come on, but have you been working out?" I glanced towards Nic. "Don't tell me you've been picking fights."

"Nothing like that," Terry said, with pride in his voice. "Running with you just reminded me that a little brawn is needed at times."

I didn't fully commit to a shrug before sitting down across from Nic.

"Did your flight make it here without any trouble?" Sonia asked.

"On schedule, and without a hiccup," Nic answered before taking a sip of his drink, which was also branded the restaurant's name in all caps. "Weirdly easy, actually."

"Russia is night and day harder," Terry grumbled after giving Sonia a hug.

My eyes stayed on him as they both sat down. "You tried to get to Russia?"

"No—"

"Yes," Nic corrected before Terry could even finish his lie.

"It shares a border with China, it shouldn't be that tricky to not leave a trail," Terry said, getting worked up. He exhaled and held a finger up to stop himself. "That's not why we are in Tokyo. How are you two?"

"Good," Sonia laughed. "You should see the house. It's a little empty right now, but otherwise perfect."

"Casio sent us some pictures. A few more freelance gigs and you'll be able to gold plate that place."

"You are vastly overvaluing my worth." I brushed a speck off the table. When I glanced back up, Nic seemed to agree, like he knew the going rate for a paid hacker.

"I'm going to go get us drinks," Sonia said. "Do either of you want anything?"

"I actually need to get something to eat, but I'll just go with you," Terry said, and stood up as well. He gestured for her to go first. When he turned, the back of his jacket faced me for the first time. It was embroidered with sakura blossoms and a skeleton.

"Terry," I called, "what are you wearing?"

They both stopped, but Sonia insisted he stay a moment longer to catch up. Terry pulled out a chair, only to sit in it improperly with his forearms hanging over the back. "So let me explain." He grinned and so did I. "Everywhere I travel now, I pick up something. Do you know the history of souvenir jackets?"

"I know nothing," I laughed. "Continue."

"Ok, so they date back to World War II. After the war, soldiers still around would get Japanese designs stitched into their jackets. Sometimes even from the threads of reused military parachutes. Anyways, Japan's youth picked up the style along with some other American clothing styles, and these jackets became a counter-statement piece and act of rebellion. Over time they worked their way into everything. From what soldiers had, to high fashion, to the Yakuza in movies. They've always been this weird souvenir, and sort of ironic badass item."

"How do you know all of that?"

"It's the Information Age. All the world's known knowledge is there for us to learn and share," Terry said. "And when it isn't in the case of UltSyn, one finds a way to expose the truth all the same."

I chewed on my lip for a second. I was trying to put all of that out of my mind the best I could. It was too hard to figure out this new life if all I did was think about the past. "Can you get up so I can see it better?"

"Sure thing," Terry said, and properly righted his chair. He stepped closer and turned around. "But afterwards I'm going to order, because I'm starving."

The jacket was two-toned like an American baseball jacket. The back had a riot of pink flowers that crossed over to the sleeves. Up close, the skeleton's hollow eyes were in the shape of mouse cursors. "You've truly outdone yourself, Terabyte."

"Thanks," Terry said with a pleased little shrug. "I'm going to see if I can catch Sonia before she finishes ordering."

Nic and I watched the silk tech skeleton walk away before I turned to him. "Did you pick up something too?"

He stared into his coffee, glanced to the side, before finally shaking his head at himself. "I did, actually." Nic leaned over to the ground, and picked up a bag. We hadn't been in Japan long, but already started to notice that it was a tourist habit. "When we went to Korea, Terry got something and I didn't. Every time I see his desk I regret not getting something." He slid the bag over to me. "So, this time I did."

I raised a brow, but silently reached into the bag and pulled out ceramic figures. The first was a black dog-like creature with a fire mane and accent on the paws. His teeth were sharp, but the big eyes and tongue sticking out made it anything but fearsome. The second matched the first, aside from an expression change of a wide smile and fangs hanging down. "These are actually really fucking cute."

"Right?" Nic said. "They make me smile."

I carefully placed them back in the bag. "Do they have some historical or pop culture meaning?"

"Not a clue," Nic said so deadpan that it even made him chuckle a bit.

<chapter five>
<! -- Scott -->

"Eat me!" Sonia grinned, wiggling a fork in my face as if her meal were talking to me. Black dots made up Domo's eyes and he had carefully cut out sharp teeth. Whatever he was made of had an unnerving brown fuzz appearance.

"No thanks. I don't even know what it is."

"Come on," Sonia said. "After everything don't you trust me?"

"Not with this." I laughed.

"Sushi wrapped with aburaage." Sonia took a bite out of the bear, monster, thing. "Or maybe it's secretly natto."

My groan was deep, primal, and from the gut. "See, that's why I don't trust you with food."

She shrugged and went back to her bento box. "The place in front of the Tsūtenkaku tower has blowfish."

"I have been missing the danger in my life."

"We should go tonight."

I raised a brow. Trying things simply because I could had never been my style. Especially when I already felt like I was faking making this work in the first place.

"To the tower, I mean."

"Oh! Yeah, I'd like that."

**

"You're being selfish. They're in love. Don't take that away from them."

I woke up a few hours later, confused about who was speaking. The room was dark and I sat up to see Sonia's face lit by the glow of her phone. "What are you watching?"

"A show," she said. I could have figured out that much. "Are you ready to go out?"

"Yeah, let me run to the bathroom first."

I headed downstairs on autopilot until I splashed water on my face. I don't know if it was coldness or the breath I took as I looked at my dipping face in the mirror. Sometimes I had to take a moment to realize that this was my life now.

When I stepped out, Sonia was waiting for me in a black sweater that slipped off one shoulder. A small smile appeared and she held a hand out for me, and I suddenly couldn't picture a night I'd rather have.

As we walked to Shinsekai, Sonia info-dumped to my delight. This area was modeled after New York and Paris, and I think that's why I was drawn to moving nearby. "There's a shooting gallery down here, I could practice some more," Sonia teased. I could tell in how she squeezed my hand first.

"Wait, is it the sort where you can win prizes?" Our place was so empty, even liberating a ten-cent goldfish would be nice. "Maybe we should."

An empty rickshaw sat in front of a building. I didn't know where the runner was, but I didn't feel comfortable being toured around a neighborhood I lived in anyways. This area was a riot of color—definitely had an amusement-fair feeling that other parts of the city didn't.

"I'd like to work up to Spa World sometime," Sonia said. I glanced around to see if we had passed it or if she was just bringing it up but nothing relevant was listed in English. The idea of being naked around strangers horrified me, even if covered in mud, but to each their own. "And get a better view of Tsūtenkaku."

The tower was currently glowing a pastel blue; the very tip was white, which meant tomorrow would have fair weather. I was glad we had waited until dark; this place was humming with lights that would have been lost in the daytime. "The lines are a bit long right now—do you want a private showing?"

"What are you planning?" She tried to keep a straight face but failed.

Sneaking somewhere we weren't really meant to be was just exciting enough without risking anything. I ducked down the side of the building, but to suggest we were out of sight was far from true. Nonetheless, I started climbing a service ladder up.

The city view was limited compared to the observation platform, but meant more to me. Sonia filled my view. The ends of her blonde hair glowed against the tower's light. My focus shifted to the words running up the sides, a sponsorship from a tech company. One that naturally leaned towards the cultural belief that there was a soul in everything. Including literal hardware. The perspective shift made the world feel right for a change.

"You definitely belong here."

Sonia stayed turned toward the city. "I think this might be my new favorite spot."

"Shame we are trespassing."

Sonia chuckled, and backed up to lean against the wall with me. "Partners in crime."

I silently held my index finger up in the air, palm towards me, and drew a few circles in the air. *Always.*

Eventually we climbed down, because I realized I hadn't eaten today and the air was thick with the dinners from a dozen or more restaurants. We could have tried out anywhere, but I really just wanted to get something out of a vending machine and keep walking around. There were plenty of them, so I could afford being picky.

When we ran into trouble again, I expected a scream to rip through the crowd. But no. It almost went unnoticed. We walked across it as casually as anything else in the world. Slumped out of the way of foot traffic was someone on their side, arms hugged against themselves. If I hadn't seen the blood smeared over his shoulder, I might have just thought he was a homeless person trying to stay warm.

Sonia instantly crouched to his level, asking for a name, asking what hurt.

Help was signed, and my stomach dropped. By standing I could see a cut along his back, towards the spine. Exactly where one might expect to find more serious UltSyn tech. I suddenly couldn't breathe. This had to be another HID. As Sonia continued to talk to him, I pulled out my phone. I called 911 because I didn't even know the number here and just hoped help would come. Some past programmer had my back, because it thankfully forwarded to Japan's 119.

<chapter six>
<! -- Scott -->

"You mean to tell me that someone is assaulting former UltSyn workers for their implants?" Otsuki asked.

"Allegedly." My comment earned me both their contempt. Maybe because they are targeted for very such things. Last night had been… stressful. "I'm not being cute. They didn't get anything so we don't know for sure what the motive was. Could have been trying to take the part out similar to stealing like an organ, or could be to sway an agenda. I just want to know what we should do about it."

"Do?" Otsuki repeated. "You shouldn't do anything unless the police call to follow up."

"Have they found any leads?" Sonia asked. Otsuki turned to face her and gave a solemn little shake of her head.

Fuck the police, I signed to Sonia; only she could see right now. It didn't win her favor, and soon Otsuki turned back. "As my lawyer, you are telling me there is legally nothing I can do?"

"Nothing you should do."

"I should also go for a run." I headed for the door where my sneakers sat.

Sonia scoffed. "Right now?"

"You heard her there's nothing to be done. Beats sitting on my hands." I tightened the laces and checked for my phone before realizing I had forgotten my headphones on the coffee table. "Could you toss me those?"

Sonia followed where I pointed, and bundled them up before pressing them into my hand. "Be safe."

I glanced over her shoulder to our guest before looking down. "I'll behave. What's the word? Uh, *yakusoku suru*." I licked my lips, too nervous to look at her. How good could my promises even be these days? There were 26 days left before my fate here was decided and I was too scared her eyes would hold a fire I once knew that reminded me to fight. "Thank you for stopping by, Otsuki-sama."

I likely should have waited for a reply, but I didn't before hitting the street. The roads around our house were narrow, and long, and as soon as my headphones were in place, I ran for it. It was easy to ignore anyone, and I only followed signs that had a blue arrow. I thought they might lead to a hospital, but actually they were for a bike path on a bigger street.

A mile or so later, I slowed at the sudden onset of trees. I was not even sure where this was, maybe the edge of a park? I walked around until I saw the top of the Tennōji Zoo, with a glass pyramid peak that reminded me of the Louvre. Before my heart rate dropped too much, I picked up the pace. Or at least as much as I could with the uptick of people around.

Between songs, there was a deep humming in my headphones. It reminded me of a pair of speakers I had that would pick up incoming texts before the phone rang. By time the song reached the chorus, the sound was gone again. I didn't think much more of it until I neared Shinsekai, and there the sound was again. White noise always sounded scattered to me; this was more deliberate, smother somehow. Maybe a whale call, but deeper.

Oh no.

What it was clicked. A 52-hertz whale was a strange animal call that the NSA used as a recruitment trap. Or at least I think it was. My nerves weren't really allowing me to remember if that was urban legend or not. My heart was at an odd crossroads of wanting to be found so I could go home, and escaping.

I ignored everyone's face and went straight for the shoes in an impromptu game of spot the fed. I did see a few pairs of penny loafers, but they were on school kids. A ruse wasn't impossible, but no one was obvious.

I looked up where the closest amateur radio shop was, since I didn't carry signal fox hunting equipment on me. If this were London, I would have kicked myself for not having what I needed, but then again it wasn't like I carried a rig on me then either. There had been no point to hunting stray signals down. *Until now.*

Scolding myself while walking there was beyond easy. I also did it while looking around the store, and standing in line. Fox hunting was a hobby of its own, and here I was, wasting money because I had the overwhelming urge to figure out something unrelated to the chaos of everything else.

The packaging went straight into the trash until I was left with a device a bit taller than my hand, with a loop antenna. When powered, the display showed bars for signal strength. I had to walk back at least five minutes before it picked up the whale call again. Without my headphones, I couldn't even hear it.

I tried to discreetly scan the area, even folding my hands behind my back to allow cyclists to pass more easily down the narrow alley. Between closely placed buildings was a domed roof that hid the sky and made me lose what time it actually was. The scanner said the signal was the strongest in front of an arcade that read *King of Kings*. I was instantly greeted by an assorted mix of retro video game sounds. Text flashed everywhere, from character profiles to high scores. Finding anything relevant here might be as hard as finding a machine set to free play.

After walking around in the arcade, I was still clueless, and wished for some mysterious person waiting for me with the answers. My silhouette in a machine's not-true-black screen held my attention for a second before I glanced back at the full bars. *What now?*

Cheering pulled my attention up as two people playing a crane game won something. Maybe I was wrong about this whole thing. Maybe I should just try to have fun like they were. The scanner in my hand beeped. I glanced down and the signal dropped.

I was on the street again without even thinking about standing up to investigate. Full signal again. A Billiken statue, which I had ignored the first time since there are so many in this part of town, now had a cat lying across his feet. Its thick collar had a black box a few inches long. That had to be what was transmitting the signal.

"Hey, kitty. Can I have that?" I reached my hand out. Solving the mystery was worth a scratch, but the cat just raised their head for pets. When I unclicked the collar, the cat jumped off the shrine.

As the cat trotted off towards a restaurant, I popped open the box, which had a battery and circuit board inside. I put the rig down so I could turn off the transmitter, and the devices stopped talking to each other. *That solved that, sort of...*

Both the signal and Billiken were Americana, so I couldn't shake the feeling that this message was for me. It couldn't just be a coincidence after yesterday either. But unless I wanted to kidnap the cat and wait for their owner, I was out of crumbs to follow.

I headed back home with the rig in one hand and the little transmitter in the other. I wasn't even home for a second before I heard, "What is that?"

"Hi, honey, I'm home." I said rolling my eyes as I awkwardly worked on pulling my shoes off with my hands full. "It's fox hunting equipment. It's uh, a way to find the source of a signal, and I did. Brought me to an arcade, where I found a cat with this."

Sonia stared. "Are you kidding me?"

I glanced around the house, wondering if I'd missed something. Otsuki-sama had left, and I didn't see a broken window or anything else I had been oblivious of. "I don't understand what the problem is."

"People getting jumped on the street and you come back with…" She gestured towards the equipment in my hand as I set them on the counter. "Toys."

"There was someone miles from our house sending out a 56-hertz whale call for me."

"For you? Otsuki-san said to do nothing." She shook her head and started up the stairs. "I knew you wouldn't just leave it be."

"I…what?" I started after her but stopped at the bottom step. "Are you mad at me because I found something to investigate on my own, or mad that I didn't do what you wanted?"

"You are making this whole situation about you," she said from the top step, before turning into the bedroom.

"I'm really not!" I called up, more defensively than anything else. I glanced at the transmitter for a moment before following her upstairs. Sonia was lying on the bed, her back turned away from the door. "Maybe it's an SOS. I can't directly help people hurt by UltSyn, but this seemed like an opportunity to help someone that needed me."

She looked over her shoulder to me, lips pressed tightly together. "Can we not talk about this?"

"Okay." I sat down on the bed, my legs stretching out on the floor. Last year I knew exactly what I wanted. It might have been self-destructive, but still. From this side of the bed, I could easily see the sliding paper doors across the landing. "Do you know what you want to do with the tatami room?"

Sonia flipped over, looking pleased for the first time since I've been home. "Thinking about tea sets, so we can have a more traditional receiving room. And a few books so there's always something to read, and, what?"

"Nothing." I tried to shake the smile off my face. "It's nothing. Just you have the same look you did at Tsūtenkaku."

"You belong here, too, so please stop looking for trouble and just stick to what's already on our plate."

I glanced back to the room across the hall that could serve so many purposes someday. *Someday* was a word that held both painful and hopeful feelings. "Alright, but you gotta scoot over. You're hogging the bed."

<chapter seven>
<! -- Scott -->

Days slipped away as the news fell into predictable cycles. Even the "breaking" news wasn't a surprise, since the thing about paying attention early is that by the time everyone else is paying attention, you're at your *breaking* point.

Everything I had to say had been said ad nauseam. Well, what I *could* say. What I was allowed to say without making too many waves. Speaking out has its limits. There's a point no one wants to talk about, when people stop listening and start stuffing your mouth with their intent. One out-of-control spin was that I was against *all* technology and that UltSyn was simply a symbol of it. That conspiracy theory could end up re-hurting everyone involved and my attempts at a more traditional livelihood.

"Hey, can you do something for me?" Sonia called from downstairs.

No. My thoughts knee jerked from an overtired place of wanting to be left alone, when the reality was that I always wanted to help. I looked up towards Sonia and managed a smile when she came up. "Yeah sure, what do you need?"

"Wait, never mind." Sonia ignored me in favor of the pliers sitting on top of a box. "Your gig is in an hour, right?"

"Uh…" I laid back on the bed to reach up towards the nightstand and my phone to check the time. "Just about."

"Good thing I don't need help after all. The JR can be a pain."

"I got a pass so it isn't so bad. If I mistranslate something, I just go back and swipe it again without needing tickets."

"I thought you couldn't get those inside Japan. Please tell me you didn't cheat the rail system."

I stared at her for a second; chewing me out for bending the rules was a new look on her. "No, dearest," I said and pointed at myself. "Temporary visitor."

"Oh." She glanced down to the pliers in her hand, and I wondered what she was going to use them for but didn't ask. I likely should have, since we accidentally got on this anxiety-filled topic. Instead, I pulled on a jacket and hopped on a different train of thought. "Casio is in town, isn't he? I was tempted to call him for some backup."

Sonia blinked up, thankfully looking a bit more amused. "Do you need backup?"

"Not really, but it's more fun that way."

"You could take me." I was almost ready to accept when she quickly spoke again. "Next time, I mean. It's nice to be partners in crime."

My chest tightened with an odd tangle of emotions that I just wanted to call good and move on. So I did. "Next time," I agreed, and signed *I love you* as I left.

***

I waited in line behind others who mindlessly scanned or paid for tickets at the automated booths. This repeated across several lines, but one woman caught my attention as she held her acrylic nails up to the scanner. The reader changed from yellow to green as it opened the divider to let her in, just like normal. I almost missed my turn trying to see how she pulled that off.

Once inside, I glanced around hoping to ask, but didn't spot her in the crowd, so I worked on paying attention to characters that slowly were growing familiar, wishing for a shared alphabet again. Huge cities were easy enough to find and usually labeled in both Japanese and English for hopeless tourists. Especially if you didn't care too much where in the city you ended up. But today I had to find a specific station that held the headquarters of a startup that was somehow both unprofitable and worth over a billion dollars. The tech field is full of financial dualities.

I found the terminal I wanted before the train arrived, which was definitely a perk. Part of the test was that they didn't know when I was showing up. I sat around for about five minutes before I spotted those acrylic nails and jumped up to follow.

"Sumimasen," I said as I jogged to catch up to her. She glanced up, noting me as if I wanted to squeeze past her, but instead I stopped. "Hi, um, how did you scan your nails?"

Her expression shifted to an uneasy smile, and my guess was she didn't speak English. *"Sumimasen,"* I repeated since I couldn't remember another apology. I held my hands up, the nails facing out. The woman uneasily mirrored me slightly before it became clear.

She flipped her hands around with a smile so I could see under her long nails. Under the index finger was a tiny silver chip. A piece of tech my pass did not have.

"Oh, uh, *kashikoi*!"

The woman smiled when I called her clever and I was doubly pleased at remembering last Wednesday's word of the day. I bowed, and said thanks before excusing myself.

I hadn't gone far, but wrongly assumed my ride wouldn't be so exact in its arrival time. With a sigh I found a spot out of the way and texted Casio: *I missed my train because I was distracted by a lady, how's your day going?*

Same phone, who dis?

I rolled my eyes and the next text message came.

Day is boring, what was interesting about her?

The clicks on my phone got a few glances so I took a second to silence my phone before continuing. *She broke open her card, took the chip and glued it on a fake nail so she always had the card on her.*

Cute, wish I could pull that off.

I grinned while picturing it. *Wanna cause some sponsored trouble?*

The train came and I felt my phone vibrate a moment later but didn't pull it out until everyone stopped funneling into the train. *Probably, what's it gonna cost to meet up?*

It was endearing that Casio seemed willing to travel for me, but I could do better than just paying for his fare. *We can split the take.*

A quick buzz followed. *Was expecting dinner, address plz.*

I sent the reply off, and then had the itch to text Sonia, but I couldn't think of a thing to say. So I just sat there until the ride was over and could distract myself by walking the rest of the way.

Less than a block away, two hands grabbed my shoulders. I seized up for a second, forgetting to exhale as I spun around to see who it was. "Jesus fuck, Casio. You scared me."

He laughed, or continued to laugh, which caused me to slug him in the arm. "Ow!" he cried, still far too amused for it to be really believable. "Building on the corner, yeah? In-person shit normally gives me hives, but white hats aren't illegal, so this should be fun."

I stopped in the tiny parking lot, mentally comparing how different it looked from the stitched-together photos that were now in 3D in front of me. Not much had changed besides the cars parked, and the paint was a duller shade.

"Do you have an ID for me?" Casio asked.

"Nope." I didn't offer any other info until he gave me a look that silently screamed *come on, please.* "I don't have one either, since they don't use them. Something about them being too corporate feeling."

"Which means that lady's nails have better tracking of who comes and goes," he said, glancing back at the building. "Gotta list that as a security threat."

"The president is a very open-source kind of guy. Doesn't worry about security too much because of his beliefs on the subject. However, their lead engineer is a security freak. I think the owner is pranking to prove a point." I walked up and held the unlocked door open for Casio. "After you."

He shot a curious look my way before falling into an act for the receptionist. Casio spoke to the lady far more fluidly than I could muster, and by his body language and the few words I knew he said something like, "This is Scott Gris, I'm his translator. We are here to see Mr. Sato." He must have researched that on his way over, because that was the name of our target.

She replied in kind and took us to a waiting room behind her reception desk. The back wall was decorated to match the social-media lifestyle vibe the website was trying to pull off, with their logo floating around with cartoon clouds. The wall in front was solid glass that looked over the desks in the middle and three offices at the back.

"Now what?" Casio asked as the receptionist left. "I assume Mr. Sato isn't actually waiting for us."

"You see the office that has the blinds pulled on the far right? That's where we need to go."

Casio sat down so it wouldn't be so obvious that he was casing the place. "Oh...kay. But, how do we get there?"

It was a Friday night, so only a few workers filled the building. Three monitors were glowing around the room. Since Casio's lie worked without question, Mr. Sato must be around, but I didn't see him, which made exploring a bit risky.

I glanced up to white soundproofing squares, the type that often hid a crawl space for maintenance of pipes, wires, and really anything else that could be tucked away for better aesthetics. Being in a modern glass box of a waiting room didn't give us much cover. There was a hanging bubble chair if you wanted to embrace the whimsical design, but it only offered slightly less cover than the more traditional furniture.

Where was somewhere private but also public that we could go? Across from the door we came in was another door to a bathroom, and I was willing to bet the ceiling was uniform. "Come to the bathroom with me."

Without question Casio followed. I think he was looking for any Raspberry Pis that were reachable and therefore hackable. "Let me give you a boost," I said, pleased that I was right.

"What?" he said and glanced up. After a sigh, he climbed up on the sink and I gave him a boost higher so he could slide the tile up and out of the way. His hand caught a pipe and he pulled himself up into the ceiling.

I think he was in the tail end of a maintenance area rather than an air vent, but I couldn't be sure until I was up there myself. I climbed on the sink, thankful for every inch of height I had and Casio's help.

Dust kicked up and I turned my head to stifle a cough. Casio sat on a metal bar waiting for further instructions, and since I was just winging it, I crawled forward in the direction of the offices. It should have been a straight shot, but this area was tight and lacked any openness that gave you bearings, unlike the rest of the building.

If we wanted to continue going straight, a bunch of ethernet cords hung in our way. I said a silent prayer that they were all clicked in securely before I pushed them as far as I could out of the way and climbed over.

"If I get stuck," Casio whispered, "we aren't friends anymore."

"Oh please." I crawled until we hit a dead end. Below us should be the engineer's office, but I wasn't absolutely sure. If it was anyone else's office we'd have to explain why we broke in. Hell, even if it was the correct office and he was inside, we'd ruin the whole job.

I awkwardly put an ear to the tile, bracing myself on the metal railing, but the soundproofing was doing a good job even from this side. A heard a sneeze and looked up to Casio fighting off another.

"What's the end goal?" He sniffled.

"We need to be able to change the guy's screensaver."

He mouthed the last word as if repeating it would cause it to make sense. "I don't understand how rich people spend their money."

I struggled to hear his hushed words, then shrugged. It was a non-harmful way to show you had accessed someone's computer. Sure, screensaver settings weren't sensitive systems, but it proved a point.

When I was a second away from texting Sonia for an idea, one came to me. "Do you have a lighter?"

Casio dug around, his leg nearly ending up on my lap as he reached into his pocket. He handed me a hybrid lighter and pocketknife, and I moved closer to the smoke detector that was poking down through the tiles.

It held the open flame there for a good thirty seconds, but I think the cold air wasn't allowing for the heat to be picked up. I used my other hand to help insulate it, and a loud screech started seconds later.

Casio had the advantage of covering his ears, as it took me a bit to get repositioned, and by that time he must have decided it was safe enough to pull the ceiling tile up and look inside the office.

He gave me a thumbs up before jumping down. I followed after he took a step away, and I started dusting off my clothes. "Oh shit, he was in here," Casio said, as he pulled himself closer to the desk while in the engineer's chair. His casualness turned into a scramble for the mouse as the computer seemed to pause. The mouse wiggled around and the screen stayed awake instead of locking the workstation.

I leaned in over his shoulder. "Is that a lab watch program?"

Casio was a click away in the personalization settings to change the screensaver when I mentioned a desktop icon. "Yeah, they used it on campus sometimes."

The words underneath, I couldn't read, but the logo was the same across country lines. "Change all the screensavers instead of just this one. If the president doesn't know about this privacy leak, he will now."

Casio started working on it, while I wished the blinds weren't closed. It made it hard to see if anyone was coming back. The alarm was still going but would likely stop soon, since the heat source was gone. I moved to the door, locking it before I peeked through the blinds.

"What are we supposed to write?"

"Uh, hold on." Now I was digging in my pockets for a scrap of paper I wrote on with the requested message. I translated it on my own time and, if I got it right, it said, "Ito owes me a beer."

"Can I change this to say us?" Casio asked. "Since it's on multiple computers now." His voice briefly boomed as the fire alarm dropped off.

"Love it, do it, then let's get out of here." A few seconds later I heard Casio get up from the rolling chair while I watched through the window as workers started trickling back into the building. "Yep, now would be good."

"This is some spy shit." Casio swung the desk chair around so he could stand on it.

"Move before it becomes 'Cops.'" We climbed back up the same way we did in the bathroom, only this time we crawled faster since we knew where to go. Casio led but called back to me. "How are we going to explain why we didn't go outside for the fire alarm?"

"Say we were in the bathroom."

He shook his head and just kept going. One shoulder leaned in more and, before I even realized what was going on, the tile broke and we both tumbled down with it. The pile we landed in was just inside the bathroom, and missed the sinks or anything else that could break our fall, for better or worse.

Casio rolled onto his back gasping in air, but otherwise looked undamaged. My arm stung, but it was more pain from an old injury instead of a new break. "Least you didn't get stuck?"

He laughed then coughed a fit before sitting up. "You okay?" he asked as I was testing my elbow. When I nodded, he added, "What does this job pay again?"

"Just dinner." I stood up, thankful that crawling around again seemed off the table.

Casio held the bathroom door open, and knew he dished it out earlier. "With friends like you…"

The waiting room was still empty, and thankfully the mess we made was unseen, so I just continued walking and decided I wouldn't stop until I was outside. Casio said something to the receptionist on our way out, but it couldn't have been much.

"You should have seen her expression," he laughed before taking a huge breath of fresh air.

"What did you say?"

"That we left a message with Mr. Sato and will check back in later."

"Solid." I glanced around, feeling like I'd lost my bearings when the ceiling fell out from under us. "Now which way is home?"

Casio wrapped an arm around my shoulder. "Let me buy you dinner first, for reminding me that life can be an adventure."

"And because the Hello World Hacker has a good going rate these days?"

"And because the Hello World Hacker has a great rate these days," he repeated and guided us away from the station. It seemed unfair that he knew my city better than I did.

"You deserve some of the credit. Did raiding a building at the end with me gain you much fame?"

"Not really. Caught the attention of a few headhunters, but didn't like their placements. I did gain a new appreciation for all the legwork you've done." He whistled loud enough that it hurt my ears. "It is always kind of fun, but I'm quite content working from home. Hey, do you like sushi yet? There's a good place up ahead."

I had been avoiding forming new opinions since I doubted they'd matter for long. But with Casio acting like a co-worker who wanted to get something after our shift, life almost felt normal. "Not really, but I'm willing to try again."

<chapter eight>
<! -- Scott -->

"So that's how much those ceiling tiles cost," I said over breakfast a few days later. Sonia looked up from a newspaper, to the letter in my hand, then finally to me with a funny little expression. "You know that job I brought Casio on last week? When we were sneaking around and shit we broke something worth 23,000 yen... a piece."

"As you do," Sonia mused. "Do you have to pay for it?"

"No, but we did get someone fired. Turns out the president didn't know his lead installed surveillance software on all the machines and let him go for 'not being the right personality fit for the company.' Guess that isn't always a bullshit line."

"Sweet, we can use that savings for tickets." Sonia started to clean up, taking her mug and plate over to the sink before continuing. "I thought since we have a free day we could go to Disneyland. Nothing says America wherever you are like Mickey Mouse!"

Her excitement was strained, and, unless she'd started watching Disney movies while I was sleeping, I couldn't imagine she had even a partial fondness for them. "I thought the train made you as paranoid as it did me."

"We could take a car."

I brought my dishes over, unfinished, but I didn't want any more. "We don't have licenses."

Sonia tossed the paper down. "You know what I mean."

"Do I? I don't know why you suddenly want a four-hour trip to a theme park neither of us have ever mentioned."

"Your visa expires today," she said as if I haven't thought about it for every second of every day since I got it. "I wanted something fun and exciting so we didn't spend the whole day worrying."

"Aww, that's so sweet, you tried to distract me with Disneyland." I wanted to pull her into a hug, but opted to drape my arms around her shouldersFst. "All I really want is to play house with you for another day, and maybe figure out who was playing the 52-hertz signal so it doesn't haunt me for the rest of forever."

She squeezed my hand, and I wondered if Casio would visit more often if I had to leave. Maybe she'd just get a new job and dedicate herself fully to it. If Otsuki-sama remained on as my lawyer, I'm sure she'd give me updates about Sonia. I sighed. These thoughts were spiraling out of control. "What would you want to do?"

"I want to help you hunt your white whale."

"If that isn't a scary comparison, I don't know what is." Our living room had a storage ottoman and I'm pretty sure the rig and transmitter got stuffed in there. I sat on one section and pulled up the cushion of another to find both pieces. Off, but intact.

"You said you found it on a cat?"

"The collar, yeah."

Sonia pulled out her phone, and I watched her type something before looking back at the equipment, knowing as sure as day there was no way to track this back to its owner without taking out the tiny circuit board and praying for a non-standard maker's mark.

"Years back there was a guy who put a memory card on a cat's collar and was pranking the police."

"That's cool." I held the transmitter up close to see how small the screws really were.

"He got eight years in jail for death threats."

I stopped cold. "Sonia!"

She held the phone out, even though I couldn't see anything besides a photo of a cat on top. "That's what it says."

"Do you, or don't you, want to do this?"

"No, no, I do."

I got up to get a screwdriver and she instantly took my seat. Buying more furniture likely counted as playing house, but that was not how I wanted to spend my possibly last free day. I ran upstairs since I thought the toolkit was left in the tatami room.

"You didn't let me get to the helpful part," she yelled up. "They figured whodunit because the police offered three million yen for information. And poof, CCTV footage of the guy and the cat turned up."

I reached into the room, grabbing everything just in case something else was needed later, and started back downstairs. "So all we have to do is hack the CCTV feeds and, ta-da, our answer."

"Simple enough." She sounded pleased, but as I reached the bottom step she understood the problem. *"Oooh."*

"Exactly."

"We could just head over to that area and see if we can find anything."

It was a heavily trafficked area, so unless they were hiding out in one of the stores and only now wanted to be found, I didn't think going back would help anything. And if it was an SOS signal, it was so long past due to offer help from anyone. "Do you know if there's been any more attacks on former UltSyn workers?"

Her face grew grim; the answer clearly wasn't a good one. She got up and I accompanied her to our bedroom. Under a slowly growing pile of clothes, she fished something out and wordlessly handed over a scrapbook.

Inside were newspaper clippings or printed articles about "strange muggings". The first was dated just before we arrived. A woman who was grabbed shortly after a train ride and was found with a wound on her head.

I flipped the page. The next story mentioned Shinsekai and I knew it had to be the guy we found. The page across from it was a tiny follow up and couldn't have said anything of value. On the third page, I spotted the characters for *dead* in the headline and kept looking.

The rest of the book was thankfully empty but the tightness in my chest eased up a little. Only three people so far. *Only.* What a sad thought to bring any sort of relief. "Why didn't you tell me?"

She didn't say anything, instead waiting until I looked up to meet her eyes. *You know why,* she signed. I gave the book back. Her hand movements had weighed heavily, but it wasn't as if the sound would have been any more bearable. How was I meant to pretend to have any sense of calm when this was happening?

I sat against our bed with my elbows propped on my knees. "The dates, when was that last one?"

"Twelve days ago." She moved to sit down next to me, either for comfort or so I could look at the book some more.

I reached over, flipping between pages for any sort of pattern. In each reported case there was violence, but no one lifted tech, so we might be the only people suspecting they were targeted for living with UltSyn tech. "The only connection to anything is that I first heard that signal a day after the second attack in the same area. It's honestly weak at best."

"If the others had something similar happen," Sonia said, "we have no way of knowing."

"So the theories are, if it was just only the second person, then it was related to that specific person. If it happened every time, it was a taunt."

Sonia shrugged a little. "Or an SOS each time. Could even be just a red herring."

"That doesn't include the idea that I was even meant to find it." That's it, I was taking the transmitter box apart. I detached the battery and removed the two screws and held the board down all within under a minute.

"Anything?"

"Nothing." I glanced up at Sonia and just shook my head. "No secret messages. No strange logos to follow. All I can think to do is turn it on and let whoever find us."

"Couldn't someone," she started falsely, needing a second. "Aren't addresses normally considered public information?"

"Unless Japan has extra privacy laws, they almost certainly know where we live already."

"I don't like it."

Couldn't say that I did either. The goal had been to be transparent instead of giving the appearance that we were hiding. I put the transmitter down because Sonia's stare made me anxious that it would come to life and bite. *Vzzzzzt, vzzzzzt, vzzzzzt.* I looked over my shoulder, to parts that were threatening to make a horror story reality when the… vibration continued. "Oh Jesus, it's only my phone."

"It's our lawyer." The caller ID made me miss the idea of murderous hijackers over the range of possibilities that would open and close after this single phone call.

Answer it, Sonia signed. Quick, impatient.

"Hello?"

"Hello, Mr. Gris," Otsuki-sama said with the calmness of a saint. "I have news about your visa status."

I'm pretty sure my lungs stopped working, making it hard to reply at all.

"I had hoped to hear news before this, but a few were trying to be sticklers about your working on a tourist visa while we all waited. Since that had already been pre-approved, in the end it was decided the best thing to do would be to grant you a two-year work visa. You can stay as long as you don't leave the country. It's a little unusual, but I already followed up and they aren't going to grant you a travel permit anywhere for security reasons."

My life *wasn't* over.

Sonia looked on expectantly and I just passed her the phone. I couldn't believe it. I got to stay, while someone simply threatening violence got months in jail. I could figure out the whale call. Or if someone was really targeting people. Hell, I *could* go to Disneyland. And not just as a finality.

The shock slowly turned into a tidal wave of relief. Dizziness hit me as I tried to put the transmitter back together. It gave me something to do as Sonia asked about all the details I was too floored to even think about. When the conversation continued long enough to feel steady again, I tested my luck by turning the device on.

<chapter nine>
<! -- Scott -->

I expected to wake up the next day and feel like a new man, but nothing had been planned past yesterday, as if today weren't meant to exist. And I felt worse for it. Jobs had kept me distracted and fear had kept me moving. *How does one be still?*

Not having an answer for that, I reached for my phone. Even my schedule was blank besides a tech conference this weekend, which got automatically added when Terry had texted me about it. Determined not to get out of bed yet, I opened the language app and got through two tiny lessons before Sonia came up stairs.

"Hey sleepyhead, come to the store with me?" She was standing at the door with one arm holding the other at the elbow.

That was a nervous new habit she'd been hiding before. The scrap book was hidden again, but this time in case anyone stopped by. "Have you been making runs this whole time while nervous?"

"It's nothing."

"No, it's not. Doesn't matter if it's unlikely. If it worries you, I want to be there."

"Get dressed and you can, I have the paperwork and everything."

I smiled, thinking that maybe it was a new day after all. After getting ready, I headed downstairs and even had my shoes on first. Sonia looped back for something, and I felt trapped at the door in the name of keeping our floor clean.

"Almost forgot my phone."

"Mind of a steel trap, yet still suffers from the doorway effect."

"What can I say, I'm only human."

We walked in silence to the convenience store. I likely would have gotten lost if Sonia weren't leading because of everything around us. Well, it was really just the one thing I saw from a way off. Up on a bridge was a huge sunglasses emoji with the hashtag #WeGotThis on top. With the whale call hiding in my pocket, maybe everything that stood out felt related.

"Scott?"

"Huh?" It took me a second to realize I had stopped outside the store to stare up at the sign a moment longer. "Sorry, I was distracted."

"Everything okay?"

"It's perfect." I stepped into the store, which had a little of everything. Toiletries filled half of an aisle running left to right; other half had impulse snacks before the register. In the back, a girl whose blonde hair nearly matched her trench coat was ordering something on a projected menu. "What are we looking for?"

"Just the basics."

Since that didn't give me anything to help with, I looked at the candy, both impressed and intimidated by the flavor variants of brands I thought I knew. The aisles were short, so I could easily see Sonia as she walked around picking up whatever was on her list. We always had to carry everything home, but normally didn't go together, so she'd likely make it a bigger haul with the extra hands.

After I turned down an aisle, someone leaning against the back door came into view. I stopped, blinking up at her cat ears made out of black fluff. A smirk appeared and she pushed the door open. My gut said *follow*, and I glanced over to Sonia as if needing to ask if she saw that too. Then again, if I checked alone, the only risk was to myself.

I pushed the door open, ending up in an alley. No one. In the second it took to think, a blur pushed me back against the building. I pushed forward again, but stopped since the figure had already backed up. "Well, you certainly are cat-like."

With a caution I didn't expect given the show so far, she fingered spelled, *Neko.*

Why would anyone translate my own words back? Then, I realized. "Oh, your name is Neko."

She nodded, pointed to me, and spelled, *Scott?*

"Yeah, that's me." I held my hands up and took another step to see if anyone else was ready to parkour off the roof on me. Seemed clear. "Who are you?"

My ears don't work well.

"I don't understand," I mumbled as I watched her sign. Either her ASL was limited or she straight up ignored my question. Of course a piece of fabric wouldn't work. The realization lit up my face as I started signing. *Sorry, I'm an idiot.*

She smiled all the same and her signs became more fluid. *You turned the signal back on, can I have a favor?*

The 52-hertz signal was for me, I knew I wasn't being vain. A nod showcased my missing fortitude. No questioning the details, just agreed like that. Dangerous move for someone who had to follow the law, maybe even more than most.

The door opened again and we both moved further away from it. We both settled when it was Sonia. "What's going on?"

Neko moved her hair back to show Sonia what I think was a cochlear implant from this angle. *You were UltSyn too, will you help me?*

"How did you find us?" Sonia's brows rose. "You've tracked us because you're the 52-hertz whale."

It wasn't sure if Neko has caught all of Sonia's comments or simply the last few words. *Not lonely,* Neko signed, her smile hinting at the alternative name for the sound. *Just a little different. Can you meet us tonight?*

"Tonight?" Sonia repeated. "What us?"

My choice was so definitely yes, I almost spoke and signed over Sonia.

Sonia scoffed, and refused to turn her back to Neko. *Because there's someone attacking people like us, and I don't think it's wise to meet up as a bigger target.*

We can tell you everything we know, Neko replied. She held a business card out and waited for me to take it. *Tonight. At Eight.*

I glanced at the card then outstretched an arm to hand it over to Sonia to see. *Why do you keep saying we? I don't know what you want in the first place either.*

You're the ones who made the disabling tech, Neko's signs became sharper with annoyance. *Did you really think you could destroy a system and things would carry on the way they were before UltSyn?*

That cut deeper than if she had pulled a knife. I didn't believe either of us were over the idea of before. Sonia forced a smile as she signed *eight* and moved towards the door. "Excuse us for trying to have a normal moment."

I licked my lips but couldn't think of anything to say, so just followed Sonia inside. Our walk back proved not all silence was equal. It had been comfortable before, but now all I wondered was if I was ruining what Sonia wanted. Which was... I don't even know. To stay safe, I guess.

We had put the groceries away, and Sonia had gone into the bathroom to clean up. A couple minutes later, I sat on the floor at the door because I didn't know what to do with myself. "Sonia," I called, wondering if she could hear me. "Do you not want to help Neko?"

Silence, then... "No, I do. I just don't know if I like my life being defined by this. Still, after being so for so long already."

"I understand."

"I wasn't just going to give up on them obviously." Frustration in her voice carried even though I couldn't see her expression. "I just wanted to choose the path rather than be tasked with it."

"Right," I said, even though I didn't see the difference. Hadn't we chosen this? I got up and turned the transmitter off. One mystery replaced with a different one. The business card was close by and I picked it up. It was for a restaurant in Shinsekai that did a lot of deep-fried skewers. But several in the area did, so nothing about it screamed uniquely special.

Sonia came out, her face washed and hair pushed back. I was surprised that she hadn't taken scissors to it yet.

She didn't look at me until I spoke. "Look at the bright side. I know where to take you to dinner tonight."

"I can't remember if it's one of those counter-only ones. Not sure how we are to meet up with anyone privately at one of those."

"Guess we'll find out."

Around six-thirty, we left the house, and by seven were at the restaurant. There was a line out the door waiting for food, and we stopped at the back of it. I turned on the fox hunting equipment out of curiosity more than anything else, but it wasn't picking up any stray signals.

The atmosphere tonight felt a lot more like a carnival with the influx of a busy night. All the lights and the food that was so fried I couldn't tell what it once was also aided the feeling. When someone bumped into us, I expected to see Neko instead of a duo that was just trying their best to get by.

"Let's hope the saying about cats and dinner is international," I mumbled as I checked the time.

Just as we reached the front of the line, I spotted the black cat ears sticking up in the crowd. She stopped in front of us like she was going to cut in line. *You look like tourists,* Neko laughed, covering her mouth as her hand stopped moving.

It was louder near the front of the restaurant, so I didn't even try to speak above the noise and signed back. *Happens anywhere.*

Neko signed something that seemed to be an agreement, but I didn't recognize the sign. Regional, maybe. Then she added a clear, *follow, please.*

Sonia and I glanced at each other before stepping out of line and doing just that. As we walked down the street, Neko casually picked up any business cards that were casually sitting out. If you did have a hideout around, this would make for as decent a decoy as any.

We stopped in an access street that didn't look remarkable in any way beside the surprising lack of a crowd. A single person sat knitting on the curb stood when he looked up and saw us. He seemed to say something to Neko as we neared, but I couldn't pick the words out. If they were planning an ambush, he didn't look the part. Almost veering on clueless.

"If they aren't the hijackers," Sonia whispered over to me, "they might agree to help us hunt whoever is down."

Neko's words were hidden as she stood with her back towards us. Whatever she had said, the guy wasn't pleased. He didn't say anything else, but balled the knitting up in a way I thought might damage whatever he was making.

"Uh, guys," I said, stepping around to the side of Neko. "Could you please explain what is going on before we decide to just quit whatever this is."

"My name is Seiji. This is my father's electronic store, and why I believe Neko brought you here." His English was strained, but still lightyears better than I could do if reversed. "Come inside?"

I stepped first into the small, tightly-packed shop, since it seemed better than being exposed on the street. The lack of light made the place look closed. Despite the clutter, Neko found a spot on the counter to pull herself up to sit. She looked comfortable, while he seemed awkward in his own store. There had to be something else not being said.

"You wanted help?" Sonia's tone seemed to almost accuse. Neko started signing, but Seiji's eyes raised to the ceiling as if the answer to that question was a matter of debate.

"Why are you two fighting?" I interrupted. All three of them turned towards me—Sonia and Neko likely because they were paying attention to each other and had missed what I was watching for. Neko nudged Seiji; he shook his head, but she insisted.

"Originally Neko said she didn't want some random American to come to Japan and protect all the UltSyn workers. But does seem to still want a fresh take on how to disable the implant they gave her more now," he said awkwardly, maybe thinking he was being rude.

I just stared for a second before laughing. "Okay, what's wrong with it?"

"Too loud."

"You couldn't turn the volume down?" Sonia asked.

Neko shook her head, clearly understanding some of what Sonia had said. *I signed up because I thought I wanted to hear like everyone else, but I didn't end up liking it. UltSyn forced me to keep it on and now their tech is still haunting me because it picks up really low frequencies. Even if I take the part off.*

"Like the whale call," I said.

She nodded. It's a deep tone constantly. *Hearing is better than just that. Barely.*

"You made a sonic weapon for UltSyn tech," Seiji said, his eyes hopeful while on Sonia. "And made it safely. Could you help us?"

Correcting him on that fact wasn't something I really wanted to do, so I kept my mouth shut. The two devices shouldn't be close enough to have the same risks, anyways. "We don't have access to the databases or any equipment." I stopped, remembering where I was. *Ah.* This plan had been clearly thought out, even if Neko had surprised Seiji at the end. "We can try."

The lack of overhead lights fostered a coldness in the air, but the idle electronics and diffused light from the outside made it possible to see. "I believe this was yours," I said and tossed the transmitter to Neko. She leaned forward and caught it in the air before leaning back on the counter and playing with it like a toy.

Sonia eyed me for a second but said nothing on the matter. "Before, we were able to bounce the sound off metal," Sonia said, and her hand floated over a bin of things so small they didn't even have their own packaging. "This time we'd have to target a specific piece of tech and shield it."

"What are you looking for?" I asked.

"I'm trying to see if they even have the parts to make what we did last time."

I didn't get why, but I didn't question it further. Instead, I turned to the others watching us. "Do you have any documentation about the implant? I've never tampered with one before."

"Hai." He nodded, stepping away into a small office and bringing out a dusty pamphlet you might find at the first doctor you visited after looking up the procedure. It was small but hopefully would do.

"Arigatou." I sat down on a stool I found, elbows up on the small workplace as I read. Ears work when acoustic energy is naturally converted into electrical signals, which are then identified as sound by the brain. The implant was made of three parts: a microphone to collect sounds, a processor, and an

array of electrodes. Likely these corresponded to the outer piece, the connector just inside the skull, and an array that reaches further into the ear, respectively.

My eyes went out of focus on the flyer, as all I could think was how we really needed to stop blindly testing parts like this. It didn't go flawlessly when Sonia tried before, and if I messed up now, Neko might pull out her claws.

I got up and hid my urge to pace by walking over to Sonia. "Find anything interesting?"

She looked over and shook her head. When she turned back, I leaned my head on her shoulder. "Actually, can you hand me that breadboard?"

"Which?"

"White one with the tiny holes."

She handed it over, and before returning to my seat, I stopped to pick up a resistor, LED, and a few other tiny parts around the store. I wasn't even sure what I wanted to make; I just wanted to make something.

I tried a few things, and they either didn't inspire me further or I was missing a piece for them. When I finally settled on an idea, my board ended up with a little LED that wavered a timid blue.

"What did you make?" Seiji asked softly as I tested it with a voltmeter.

He moved closer now and I glanced up to see his face. "You know how power moves in different directions? AC flows up and down, and even pulsating current has predictable waves. I was thinking about how life doesn't follow a pattern. There are an endless number of factors that can change the outcome of things. What if I hadn't found that signal? What if

I'd never turned it on again? What if we'd never even made it to Japan?"

He stared, and I didn't know if he thought I was just rambling nonsense, or if he couldn't translate my nonsense in the first place. I reached over and adjusted the power, and the light grew brighter. "The future is a variable current, and everything comes down to power."

"True, but how does that help?"

"Rubber duck this with me. The implant works by turning sound into an electrical signal. That's how brains work, too. If the sound is causing Neko pain, why can't we employ a TENS-like solution to disrupt the problem?"

Movement caught my eyes as Neko signed from up on her tiptoes. *This doesn't look like our tin hat approaches.*

"I wouldn't just stick a TENS device over your implant, but..." I inhaled deeply, really wanting this to work. "In theory, it's how I'd go about it."

"I didn't see any in here," Sonia said. "Aren't they usually in drug stores?"

Neko swirled her arm around. *Let's go.*

"Hold up, we still haven't eaten, and I have a lot of questions I want answered first. You must know something about the UltSyn workers."

Neko turned away like she didn't hear Sonia, which was a pretty weak excuse right now. Seiji rubbed his eyes. "That's because we don't know much. We checked the feeds for the attack in town, but it wasn't clear who it was. One attack was in a rural area and the other, well, the killer hadn't been taken in."

"Was the 52-hertz whale related?"

"Not really," Neko said. When I waited for more, she sighed and signed the rest. *You had called the cops, so I didn't know if you were done fighting, or not. I didn't want to ask if help wasn't available, and thought you decided to retire until the transmitter was turned back on.*

Sonia circled the topic back. "So, you don't know if it's a group or just some assholes on the street?"

"Both?"

There was a lot in that word that wasn't being directly said. But what she meant seemed clear. That hate was always organized, even loosely. I also understood Sonia's annoyance, but nothing with UltSyn ever came easy. In the months we'd been here, pneumonia or an accident was a bigger threat. But something you could see was easier to fight, and there'd never be a single bad guy that Sonia wouldn't find and stop in order to feel at peace.

"How about you call us if you hear anything else?" I said, trying to take the path that would make everyone happy. "Or if you need more help with making the device?" We traded numbers and I added it to an encrypted app instead of the contact book.

Sonia and I skipped the restaurants and just got something out of a vending machine on our way back. I could tell from the tight, two-handed hold on her sandwich that she was not happy. "Terry's traveling the world, did you ask him if he's heard of anything similar?"

"He said he hasn't." She swallowed roughly. "That's if he even knows what he's looking for."

"Sonia, come on." I crumpled up my trash and tossed it. "He's a smart man. If someone was hijacking parts from people, it would be bigger news."

"Your sister wasn't 'bigger news'."

Shit. She had me there. "Fine, how about this: it's not profitable to steal the parts from the workers, and I still don't think there's a way to get information without a willing participant."

"Then why did this happen?"

"I dunno, love. I don't know all the variables."

My phone buzzed with a motion alarm as we walked up to our door. Sonia was a step behind me, and as I pulled off my shoes, she just stood there. "I'm going to speak at that tech conference."

I froze, thinking about the logistics of adding another speaker days before the event. Then having Sonia, specifically, after we've been running on a radio silence about everything so far. "You want to be bait."

Sonia met my look, maybe even waiting for the no that was on my tongue. The *you are safe now, don't do this. Not now, not ever.* But when I closed my eyes, I knew all those words would stay trapped in my chest. It was her choice, I told myself as I took a step up.

"Wait." Sonia moved to the edge, looking so small with the increase in height difference. "You're the most-wanted hacker in the world, who has been transmitting a signal to a stranger for, what, days now? And I'm the brilliant hero. We don't need to be afraid of what's out there."

I pressed my lips tight to keep from smiling, because I didn't want to be so easily swayed. But, for the first time tonight, I didn't feel cold.

<chapter ten>
<! -- Scott -->

They say Shinsekai is the most dangerous area in Osaka, but you know you are going somewhere truly questionable when articles featuring cybersecurity tips are posted for anyone going to the same conference as you.

As it turns out, getting Sonia a speaking spot was very easy, because Terry just added her to his. My badge didn't have my name, since it was part of a set for people who accompanied him. Maybe I should take part in life last-minute more, because it was working out for me so far today.

It felt weird and also liberating to be standing backstage without any cards on me and with my phone off, since I didn't want to be the inspiration for an impromptu game of "what information we can sniff off the Hello World Hacker." No one had spotted me yet, but that was because we hadn't really shown our faces to anyone.

Besides Terry of course, who was over the moon that I got to stay in Japan. And had come to the conference after my original no. I trusted that he was personally happy for me, but I already felt like he had something cooking that he was simply too busy to talk about just then.

"Our next two speakers include Terry Clark, member of The Hive, a hacktivist group focusing on biohacking and heavily involved with the recent events in London. And our surprise guest, Sonia Larsen, a former UltSyn worker who served several years as a Human Information Drive. They are here to talk about medical device ethics."

Terry and Sonia stepped out to a small round of applause. "I know there's a lot of spectacle in both of those bios," said Terry, "but we are going to lead a topic-rich discussion, since this is a dense subject. Please also remember that we are not medical professionals, so if you get any harebrained ideas, don't be a *wee clipe* about where you heard it."

"If you needed that translated, I cannot help you there," Sonia joked. "Scottish idioms were not my wheelhouse."

Even watching them on via a small tablet with the live stream on backstage, I could see Terry grin. Sonia scanned a set of flashcards as he went on. "Projected above me is a brain scan. Five percent of murder cases now involve these scans in some sort of defense. But as evidence goes, these digital files have an obvious weakness. What if the files get swapped out? What if the device scanning was tampered with?"

"And it's not just medical files," Sonia said as she pocketed his notes. "A software program called COMPAS has been used for sentences. The company keeps the algorithm hidden for profits, but that also means it cannot be held accountable if someone secretly manipulates it anywhere from code to trial."

They were actually kind of cute. I wished I could dramatically walk onto stage and declare some fact that made the world weird, too.

"More than 700,000 pacemakers are installed yearly," Terry added as the two built up to a biotech nightmare that was sure to come. "These devices clearly save lives, but their data can be given to the police to check the story you gave them. In 2017, this method was seen at least three times in three different cases, by a single police department."

I expected Sonia to jump back in but her eyes had fallen away from the crowd. Maybe she'd stopped having as much fun as Terry was. He picked up a small device from an otherwise ignored podium. "This is a blood pressure device that I was able to hack from outside the hotel I was staying at."

There was a rumble of noise, and I was tempted to peek out so I could see the audience themselves. "I can't tell you the brand," Terry seemed to tease. "But they did say I could hand out prizes, so here." He moved closer to the edge of the stage to throw it underhand to someone who had to be in the first row or so.

"Sure, these are just a meter. But for those who have to track that stat, it can change their normal day into a run for the hospital."

Sonia held her hand out and it took Terry half a second to realize she wanted the projector controls. "X-ray machines? By default, they aren't encrypted. Log into the user station and you can swap out or delete whatever you desire." She clicked again. "These smaller devices? Run on an old version of Windows. Which means if you can hack a Windows system, you can handle this." She clicked past a screen. I think it talked about companies forcing hospitals to buy new equipment needlessly, but it didn't stay up long enough for me to be sure.

When she skipped over another section, I thought Terry was going to demand control back. Instead he just looked on, lost over what was going on. "Many medical devices can be hacked, and have been vulnerable since their creation. They are poorly secured, sometimes even opening up back doors to systems that are connected to them as well. But the real danger is to those who are at risk of being harmed by this manipulation. They could possibly be controlled by the law, an employer, or by anyone else looking to fill the role of abuser. Any questions?"

The audience made no noise; I thought Sonia might repeat the question. "If anyone has a problem with me, we'll be playing Spot the Fed."

Terry's mic picked up a hesitant clearing of his throat. "Right, if you do have questions, please come up to the mic."

"Hello, instead of the common ransomware attacks on hospitals, should everyone be on the lookout for a patient's health being remotely held hostage?" A nervous laugh rippled through the crowd as Sonia ducked backstage.

I waited only long enough for her to disconnect her microphone. "What the hell was that? And *we?*" I said and signed the word. I felt like she'd pushed me deep in and yelled *GO!* "I don't want to play find the fed."

"You don't have to. I can get Terry to play with me so I won't look so suspicious searching for someone else."

"He put together a CTF team, which we also aren't hijacking from him. We don't need to annoy any hackers or any feds who decided to come. You know I'm into your whole 'voice for the voiceless' goal, but you can't just show up randomly here and yell the whole time."

"Why not?"

"Because not everyone who desires a say wants to yell, Sonia." My voice ironically raised higher than I wanted. Thankfully it was doubtful anyone on the other side of the stage at least heard us. I took a breath and tried again. "Because not everyone wants to scream their whole life. Not when people rarely listen to the canaries in the coal mines in the first place."

Sonia looked away, reminding me of my sister when she didn't want to talk about anything anymore. "When is the CTF event?"

"I don't…" I bit my tongue and just went to get the schedule someone had left back here. Found our event, found a drone race—there, hackathon. "It's at four."

"Gives us like two hours."

"Why do you even think someone is going to try and harm you here?"

"I don't think that," Sonia said. "That's why you are here. But maybe someone will know something and forward that along."

Motherfuck, I was the bodyguard.

Since Sonia was dictating my schedule now, I just followed her. We headed out a back door, only briefly joining the crowd to head upstairs. We broke off from the group again to overlook the floor below. If I did have to defend Sonia, this was really a bad spot for it. We were in the open and locked in by foot traffic unless we wanted to join their flow.

I leaned on the railing. "I'd tell you to look for men in penny loafers, but I know you aren't actually looking for a fed." I watched what had to be two hundred people pass without getting a reply. "You should have asked Neko for that CCTV tape. We could have tried to find the guy, like we matched the height before."

"Oh shoot, that's right." She glanced over but looked to be figuring something out. "Could we still do that without Hallie?"

"Maybe. I'm sure Japan had plenty of its own social media that could be cross-referenced," I said as I heard music being played on someone's phone. The bass was dropping out a bit, but it was similar enough to catch my attention. When I started to tap the familiar pattern, I looked around for the source.

Script was standing just up the landing, and barely out of the way, with a box under one arm and their phone up playing the song we'd played the night we'd all attacked UltSyn. "Miss me?"

"Ahh, you're in Japan!" They met me halfway. "I thought—never mind. I'm excited to see you."

"Sorry for the show. I didn't want to scare you." Script placed the box on the ground before giving me a hug.

"No complaints from me."

Script and Sonia hugged before they picked up the box again. "With her help, I got you a housewarming gift. I know it's a bit late for the actual home part, so consider it a congrats-on-getting-to-stay-in-Japan gift."

I looked over to Sonia, who smiled again, clearly involved in this random nice thing for me. The package wasn't wrapped and it opened as easily as a shoe box. I took a second to stare at tissue paper and thought they might actually be shoes. High top Converse, actually, with the American flag on it. "You're killing me." I laughed and pulled one out to realize the flag was actually upside-down. "Oh my god. I love these."

"Was looking for something that reminded you of where you've been while also noting where you are," Script said.

"It was so weird when they asked me your shoe size awhile back," Sonia said, and took the box from me. "This rivals my white hat gift."

"Aw, you should have reminded me to wear that today," I said, and sat down so I could put on the shoes. The stars were over the heels, and stripes ran the rest of the length. "Truly would have completed this whole outfit."

Sonia handed me the other shoe and put my old ones in the box to avoid carrying them around all day. "I thought you couldn't make it, Script. What are you doing here?"

"Yeah, I had some passport concerns and almost just gave up, but Terry promised it would be like a reunion so." They made a click sound and shrugged. "What are you guys up to? Just hanging out up here?"

"I think someone is trying to steal UltSyn tech while it's still being used in person," Sonia said. As if reminded further, she looked back over the ever-moving crowd

"Heavy." Script stared off, blinking a few times. "Never a dull moment with you two, is there?"

"Sonia crashed Terry's talk earlier."

"I did not crash," Sonia said without looking back.

"Uh-huh."

"Maybe... I should go check on him?" Script asked, clearly uncertain of the choice. "When can I meet up with you guys later?"

"You aren't a part of his CTF team?"

"Nah, I think he's using it to recruit."

"Sonia promised we could head over there in a couple hours, so we can meet up then?" At my words, Sonia gave me a look that clearly said *I did not promise.* I ignored it.

"Please stay out of trouble until then," Script said as they started to back into the crowd. "Oh! And remember don't connect to the free Wi-Fi here."

"Why? Did you do something to it?"

"Only me and probably a dozen other people."

I shook my head and started people-watching again. Someone did actually stand out. He had sunglasses and a phone to his ear. I walked over to the other side to follow his path a bit longer. Huh, I'd actually found a fed. Or at least someone I'd tell the person running the event about. "What are we actually looking for again?"

"Just someone suspicious."

"We are at a hacker convention. Everyone here is suspicious."

"Ugh, fine, we've been up here too long without any success anyways."

Sonia felt her pockets and came up empty. "Do you still have that schedule?"

"Nooope."

"Shoot, it's fine. I think I saw some downstairs."

I followed her and got bumped around a little as the convention hall got more filled as the day went on. In between escalators was a large map that had a bunch of programs in a plastic pocket. Sonia picked up one and started flipping. "Oh hey, there are rules in here."

I just shook my head and let her go on since she wasn't paying attention to me anyways.

"The dude we need to talk to is in a lounge downstairs."

No point asking who or why. "Show the way."

Sonia was a little hard to keep up with since she'd squeeze in between people I would have just waited for. Maybe I had grown more reserved since coming here. Five *excuse me's* later, we were outside of a food court. It was nicely tucked away as its own thing, instead of a last-minute addition on rolling food carts.

"I may have not spotted the fed," someone said. I turned towards the sound since it was far louder than it needed to be. The guy in the way of traffic was with another person. It was unlikely they were feds themselves given their name brand fake disheveled look. When he knew he had my attention, he continued: "But I did find a murder."

"They will let anyone in these days," I joked nervously, and tried to shuffle on ahead, but this area was full of people trying to decide which line they wanted to be in, and so had slowed to a near halt.

"Maybe he is a fed now," his friend said. His accent was a bit thicker and clearly pegged them both as Americans. "How else did he get away with everything and be granted a work visa? Dude made a deal."

"Don't call me that." I don't know why that sounded so wrong to my ears when Script's saying guys didn't.

"What do you two want?" Sonia said, stepping forward as if she was so sure these were the right type of bad guy she was looking for.

"I say we get An to vote on it. Fed or not."

I'm not sure what the host was called but that sounded a butchered version of a possible name.

"How about you leave us alone?" Tension was growing and the traffic around us bubbled like it instinctively knew. That combined with the mixing of food smells, and I was getting sick.

"Leave her with us and we will consider it," the first fuckboy said.

Sonia scuffed. "Here I was hoping you were a different type of asshole. Come on, Scott, let's go." She grabbed my hand and pushed her way through and didn't stop until we were outside the convention hall. "Are you okay?"

I didn't know how to answer her right now. I took a breath and reminded myself we actually were okay. "Yeah, just miss the anonymity I had before at these types of things. Now I'm someone who did that thing, and everything is up for debate. How can I even be me when I know one wrong move and it will reflect back on others?"

"I hadn't considered that." Sonia's words weren't a magical fix but they still soothed. "I feel responsible to my... community in a different way."

"I know, and I think it makes sense," I said. "It's a smaller group, and the dynamics are different. Or at very least not so set in stone yet."

"I guess that's true." A few people stopped to gawk at us, but they had the grace to leave us be.

"Maybe you were right," Sonia said, wiggling the toe of her shoe over something on the ground. "Maybe the attacks were just hate crimes."

I pulled Sonia close, holding her in my arms for a moment. Despite the level of PDA it might count as. "I'm sorry I don't have the answers."

She turned her face up at me. "I never expected you to. Maybe we can put this behind us and go root our friend on?"

"I'd like that."

We found the CTF game in an open room, with dozens of computers spread around the various teams as they digitally hacked the other team's flag or tried to defend their own. Terry was too busy to even notice us, and I didn't recognize any of his team, so I figured standing near Script was best. Even if we were spotted again, I was close enough to people I trusted with my life that it mattered less to me.

Hackers doing their thing isn't exciting to watch unless you like that sort of thing. Which I do, but even still it's mostly just standing around and feeling pride when someone you care about does something smart. Like sports, actually. By the end, Terry's Hive scored enough points to place second. He was playing it sooo cool when he conceded, I wondered if this was also a recruitment ploy.

"Make any new friends to help your noble cause?" I teased as he walked over.

"Got a few numbers," he said, casually proud like someone in a bar. "Speaking of causes, let's walk to my hotel room. I have something to discuss with you all." Instead of heading upstairs we headed towards the guest elevators and all piled onto what felt like a random floor.

Script was the first out and started leading us down the hall. The room wasn't too far away from the door. When Terry used a traditional key to open it, I was expecting some extra security inside, but was met with a nice but otherwise average two bed room. Script flopped down on a bed, having already claimed a side.

"Who wants to visit China?" Terry said, arms outside like he'd just pull the window curtains over and we'd realize the surprise. He was met with silence, besides the slight amused head shake from Script. "It's nothing illegal. I basically need help finishing up with the union I'm working on for the former UltSyn workers. Would be a week, maybe? You should have a say in how it's set up. Given your letter, and your obvious work experience," he said to me and Sonia respectively. Relentless is what he was. I missed that.

"It's illegal for me to leave Japan."

"Ah." He lifted a finger to tell me all the ways to get out of it, then held his tongue as if knowing I could think my own way out if I wanted. "Perfectly legal besides that."

I half-expected Terry to break into one of the rooms to help avoid the place being bugged or something or another. Maybe he wanted everything known now, maybe he really was safe enough to just casually stay in a hotel room while people knew who he really was. Legality looked good on him. All it had done for me so far was give me a new life where I wasn't sure what I was allowed to touch.

"I'll go," Sonia said.

"What?" Maybe I should have just politely looked on in surprise, but I thought we were a team. That meant being together, didn't it?

"I'm allowed to travel, so why not when the situation calls for it." Sonia shrugged, completely missing what my deal with it was.

"You were hunting for a killer like two hours ago. And now this?"

"Killer?" Terry repeated.

"Scott," Script said, from their quiet spot. I looked over, feeling a defensiveness rise until they simply patted the bed for me to sit down. It gave me something easy to do, so I sat down on the edge.

Sonia gave me a worried look before turning back to Terry. "Have you heard of any UltSyn workers being attacked? Or killed in relation to their being HIDs or anything similar?"

"I only spoke with a hundred or so—out of, what, ten thousand? I don't know everything for certain. But, no? I mean, I heard of a story where one died of exposure in the U.S.

but that's homelessness, not homicide. Is there something wrong in Japan?"

"I don't know. I thought maybe, but there are no real leads we can follow. Plus, if someone is harming others, we *should* be organized."

I hated that I didn't disagree. "When do you leave?"

"At the end of the conference."

I bit my tongue and Sonia followed up. "Could I just travel back with you and Script?"

"Oh, I'm not going," they said, sitting up more. "I already promised my time to different human rights groups, but I can stay in Japan a little bit more. Maybe give Casio shit for not coming to our little reunion."

"It's settled then," Sonia declared, and the discussion shifted to where the rest of us were, and if there was anything else at the con we wanted to do that night.

<chapter eleven>
<! -- Sonia   >

Terry's choice of music was internet radio streams. He'd randomly pick a populated city that spoke English and tune in. Our flight had been delayed right after we'd boarded, and I was thankful that he'd brought a headphone splitter.

Sure, I could have done my own thing, but I was curious if his choice of entertainment was to globally stay informed on a local scale or if he just liked changing things up. I didn't ask, because limiting it to languages you understand without further context of who owned the radio station already put a flaw in both my theories.

Once we were in the air, I dozed off and woke up to him saying something. "If it don't make dollars, it don't make sense."

My mind was still hazy from poor sleep as I sat up. Was that a lyric or a statement about something?

He glanced over. "Don't you think it's strange how a company can be around for over a decade and never turn a profit?"

The glass window to my left was dark and radiated cold. The thin blanket on my lap wasn't good for much. "Not if they are taking all the money out to pay themselves lavishly," I said, pulling the blanket closer anyways. "Or are trading in a currency that doesn't traditionally count as profit."

Terry grinned. "You have a head for this type of intrigue. Here," he said as he laid his blanket over mine.

"Aren't you going to be cold now?"

"Nah," he shrugged. "I wanted to get up and stretch my legs anyways."

When we finally landed, I expected Nic to pick us up, but I still didn't see him even after we'd arrived at the hotel. Which was surprising actually. I expected him to set up camp somewhere like Scott and I had.

To be fair, this place was nicer than some cheaper apartments. The view alone was likely worth the price. A sea of skyscrapers the same hue as the evening sky held light more than the sky currently had. There must have been countless people down there, but I could only see a steady mixture of head and tail lights.

"Nic rented the room while we were at the conference, so you can choose wherever you want to sleep. That isn't his room, obviously." He laughed to himself, and put his bags down before joining me for the view. "God, I love traveling."

"What's the agenda?"

"Uh," he scratched at his brow. "I only scheduled an organizing meeting for tomorrow since jet lag normally kicks me ass as soon as I settle. After that, two interviews and canvassing for the rest of the next day. Do you need anything? I want to get a run in after sitting for so long."

"I'm fine, ready to help now, but tomorrow it is."

"That's the spirit." He smiled, hand brushing my arm as he left the room. I rocked on my feet before deciding to wander around the room. One bedroom was open and bare, leaving the closed doors likely a bathroom and Nic's room. I ignored both in favor of the mini-kitchen.

It was emptier than Scott's old refrigerator, but thankfully I found a box of cereal bars. They weren't even the hiker variety, being half sugar.

"Shit, shit, shit," Nic said as he opened the bedroom door. His hair was unusually messed up. I titled my head towards the unmade bed and glowing computer inside. He stopped when he saw me, blinking a couple times. "You aren't Terry."

"I am not."

"Where is he?"

"Working out."

After a twitch of his lips, Nic turned back around for his room.

"Hey wait," I called after. "Is it a problem I could help with?"

"Can I send you on a mission to copy information off a computer to help figure out why our Hive accounts are being followed by a bunch of bots?"

"…I'm going to go with no."

"That's okay." He turned for his room again but ended up doing a complete spin. "Would you be willing to remotely man a drone while I look at the technical stuff?"

In my years of working for a cutting-edge biotech company, no one trained me for or even casually asked if I wanted to mess with one of those. But how hard could it be? "I would be willing."

"Cool, cool. You need to fly down to the street and over two buildings," he said, miming the directions.

I don't think I even said another word as a quadcopter was placed in my hands. In the safety of the hotel room, I practiced flying around and nearly destroyed a decorative vase in the process. The drone always dipped to one side harder than I expected, and the boost option felt super fast for half a second and then would abruptly stop.

With a bit more confidence, I went out to the balcony with my new robot friend so I could get a feel for its range. The controller had two handles on the side and a screen in the middle of what the drone saw. Inside I just watched the device itself, but as it lifted above my eye level I really didn't have that choice anymore, and I felt like I had to relearn how to fly.

It zipped up two stories fast and bumped into the glass of another room. I spun the camera around to see someone else staying in the hotel giving me—well, I guess the drone, rather—a funny look. Luckily, they were on the phone, so I quickly zoomed away towards a billboard.

"Beautiful," I said, reading the word off a large flower in a logo digitally manipulated to grow inside a phone.

"What are you two doing?" Terry asked. I didn't even hear the door from out here. He must have changed in the gym and was now in sportswear; he even had a towel around his neck.

I just looked to Nic, who had looked to me as if I was meant to answer. "Is this about the bot thing?" Terry added.

"They are a serious threat to both PR and... never mind." Nic forced a smile and reached for the snack box I'd left on the counter.

"Why never mind?" I hit recall on the drone and watched it safely come back inside before looking to them for the answer.

Nic was using the excuse that his mouth was full, while Terry rolled his eyes at the show. "Nic thought he caught the bots before, and I told him to leave it because if we wanted to stay aboveboard, we had to do aboveboard things. This is why

I asked you to be our face, to show legitimate support for our non-profit. Not to go on adventures."

"Down the street is hardly far."

"And where a CEO works. I know," Terry said as he sat on one of the bar stools. "It could ruin the cover if we actually break into places ourselves."

"You're a traveling red herring. If a target gets hit when you are in town, you are blamed but have a legit alibi. Meanwhile, the target still got hit."

"That's one way to look at it." His expression and tone gave nothing, and I told myself never to play poker with the man. "All I know is we need to mobilize people, and it's easier to do that in areas that aren't grey."

"What good is fame if you don't use it to protect others?" I asked rhetorically, but in support. "If you'll excuse me, I'm going to get some sleep for the meeting tomorrow."

I hadn't decided to take the remaining bed until right then. Not even sure my decision was anything more than making a clean exit. The bed was huge, and I likely could have even shared it if I was feeling sociable. I closed the door and just dropped my bag again, since what did it matter. After curling up on the bed, I messaged Scott that I was safe and asked how he was before starting scrolling through local news to see if anything did happen while Terry was out.

A text from Scott came in. *Having bad dreams and missing you.*

Aw sorry love, I typed back. *Miss you too.*

The Hive's pinned post was a Join Us message for tomorrow that couldn't apply to all that many of their followers since we were in China and the whole page was in

English. The rest of the messages shirted the line with playful anarchist talk.

The next day, I was dressed in my best as we piled into a discreet chauffeured vehicle. We stopped at a sprawling multi-building business complex. The view from here was less impressive than where we stayed. I wasn't sure if that was a hopeful sign or not.

We met with a Chinese woman who was fluently talking with Terry seconds after our arrival. I wanted to listen to it, but Nic's voice spoke over it.

"I'm surprised Scott let you leave." He pursed his lips. "I mean, you should be allowed to do what you wish, and I'm just surprised it collectively happened."

"We are our own people."

"Right, but you're also a team." He shrugged a shoulder, and looked forward. "For more than just UltSyn things."

A syllable of something half-stumbled out of my mouth as I instinctually glanced to where he was looking. Nothing new magically appeared besides a few more people, one of which gave Terry a friendly wave before sitting down. "I don't want to talk about this."

"Okay." As if it had never been mentioned in the first place, Nic took a seat.

I didn't know where to go, so I just followed my curiosity and sat in the front row on the side where Terry was standing. "We will give a few more minutes before we start."

I didn't know what I'd expected when I'd agreed to come, but this wasn't it. I've seen Terry with a gun in his hand, and now he had a clipboard for signups. When he pointed me out in the crowd, I nodded and smiled, but I wasn't able to pay much attention to what I'd reacted to. I swore the guy who waved at Terry kept staring at me. I tried to keep an eye on him, but he was behind me, so I could only casually take a look when someone back there spoke.

The second time I looked, he was sitting forward in his chair like he was going to reach over an empty table to tap on my shoulder.

By the end, I was too creeped out to do anything besides huddle by Terry as people broke into smaller groups. "Who is that?"

He looked over the group of forty. "Who? Oh! That's Harry. He turned over a lot of UltSyn files to the police to corroborate what we stole. Worked for them longer than you did, even." He looked to be in his fifties, so that could be true.

The groups were brought together again, and Terry called for volunteers who could take charge locally and let everyone know we'd be in Guangzhou in two days.

A woman stood and signed with a prosthetic. *I will. If Sonia still believes in you, then as an HID, so do I.*

"Wonderful, thank you."

As people started to leave, I wanted to follow her, but Harry blocked my path. "Excuse me, I'm sure this sounds strange, but I need to talk to you."

I wasn't going to go anywhere with him. "Then say it here."

"I can't stay in China long, and I hear you are moving on to a new city soon anyways, but..." Harry ran a hand through greying hair. "I think I worked with your father."

<chapter twelve>
<! -- Scott -->

And when she left, she left behind ruins. I knew this for sure because an enby was currently hunting around my kitchen unable to find a bowl to have some of our imported fruity cereal in.

"I'm sorry about the mess," I said, feeling embarrassed as my guest had to wash their own bowl. "Doing the laundry every morning I have down, but I keep thinking our dishwasher is going to hold more than it does."

"It's whatever. I haven't had to rent a hotel once since I've been in Japan, so it's beyond fine." Script leaned over to take a bite as they stayed standing at the counter, food in hand the whole time. "You do laundry, and Sonia picks up the dishes slack. Anything else I should know?"

"Uh, yeah, here's a pro-tip. If you sign like this at Casio's house," I said, showing him the sign for pizza, "you will order delivery."

It took a moment for them to realize I wasn't joking. "Ada doesn't do that here?"

"Nah, I turned it off. She has drones fly around sometimes, though."

Script walked over to sit down by me. "Mind if I ask a weird question?"

"Uh, no?"

"Why do all your AIs have feminine names?"

I didn't know if I had an answer for that. I stalled with another pointless sound or two. "Ada is named after Ada Lovelace. You know, the 'first computer programmer' and all. Hallie was a HAL joke and the default voice was feminine, so I never really thought about it."

"Good of a reason as any."

"Yeah?" I didn't know why I was equal parts comfortable and terrified talking about gender in Script's presence.

"Yeah. I was promised a tour, so where are we going?"

I actually hated the idea. I didn't feel knowledgeable enough to say here are all the important places in town. Because how does one even rate that? Especially me, who is impressed with things big or small. *Here's an abandoned shine I found while running, and over there is my favorite spot at night where you can overlook a busy street that just glows with lights from the quiet bridge above.* "Could you just tell me what you wanted to do tonight, and I can pick the best location for it?"

Script cleaned up the last bits of cereal that were clinging to the side of the bowl. "That works for me. Can you play pool? We can play for money and bragging rights."

I leaned back in my chair, pretending to try to recall a time long ago. "You know I don't think I ever have. Will you teach me?"

"Sure thing," Script said as they dumped the remaining milk into the sink. They were halfway into putting the bowl away when it clicked. "Heyyy now, you little shark."

I laughed and started to look up locations where we could find a pool table. "I haven't played while here, so if I take us somewhere shitty at least we went together."

"Fair enough." There was a small mumbled surprise as Script tried to operate the countertop washer. I heard the dish clink against another before they went on. "When was the last time you really did play?"

"Nic won 100 pounds off me." If I had expected any surprise, none came—just the comfortable reassurance of someone replying me too.

Script opted to walk to the local bar I'd found. It was my favorite time of night, where everything looked blue. "I still don't know why you didn't want to visit the pool hall in the basement of the world's largest Hello Kitty shop," I teased, since it was in Tokyo anyways.

"Yeah," Script laughed. "I'm pretty sure that's how I die."

"Please, as if a place that says 'Like pool? Like darts? Like beer? Like sports? You can enjoy all of them here' is any less suspicious."

This bar was the oldest of its kind in the area. It had classic pub-like decor and a metal loft area that had sofa seats. There were darts, a foosball table, and two pool tables, one of which wasn't taken, so we walked right towards it.

"Hey, the TV even has English subtitles on," Script said, gesturing up at it.

"Oh yeah, that's likely because we are by America-mura." I picked out a pool cue as Script racked the balls. "The area used to sell a lot of imported stuff, now it's supposedly a youth and street-culture center or something."

"And you didn't think you could be a guide." Script pointed to the table. "Break."

"I don't think you fully know the importance of those little sections of town that aren't your culture until you don't live in yours anymore." I chalked up before taking my shot. One ball fell into a pocket, which wasn't amazing but I got to go again.

"Geez Scott, you can't even break straight."

The comment had been timed just right that any reaction on my part could mess things up. And I definitely did. As the ball went nowhere useful, I laid my head down on the side rail for a second. "Fuck'n."

"All's fair in love and pool," Script said as they studied the board. They sank in three balls before I realized why I was both comfortable and afraid to be close to them. It was freeing, as if existing were never plastered over with an assumed default. Solidarity existed, but there was no safe way to tell its depth.

"Script," I said, and they just hummed a *what?* so I didn't mess them up. Accidentally or not. "Does your group work on queer issues?"

Another ball fell in. "It focuses on transgender concerns, so yes. How's Japan's scene?"

"I dunno. In America, hell even in the UK it seemed very…" I put my cue down and tried to mime what I was thinking of. "Flattened. Umbrellaed. I feel like the individual groups gather differently here. I'm not sure where I'd go if I wanted to. Probably a 'mileage may vary' situation, so I could be wrong."

Script missed the next shot, being distracted now, or maybe fate was just trying to be merciful to me. "That could have its advantages sometimes. You have fewer people to rally, but concerns from specific groups would be dropped less often."

"People are complicated," I conceded, since anything else took too much attention away from a shot that I thought could sink two balls in at once.

We played a few more rounds, and somehow I lost count of how many drinks we had before deciding to head back home. I have been drunk twice before in my life, but the third time was the charm. Maybe it was the different spirit or the world around me, but I went from having fun perfectly sober to feeling invincible. Sonia's words of we don't need to be afraid anymore played over in my head before a question from Script made me focus on the moment once again.

"Do you know how to hack that crosswalk sign?"

"Of course I do." I squinted as I looked across the street. "Wait, no, yes. They have a default click pattern."

"You can win back your money if you can make it turn green right now."

"I didn't lose any?"

"Exactly, now let's see it."

I pressed the pattern I remembered. It had made me think of Morse when I'd first learned. The red of don't walk flipped over. "Ask and you shall receive."

"Wait," Script said, looking carefully back at the button as we crossed. "How do I know that wasn't just lucky timing? Change the streetlight or something."

"One, no. Two, that tech uses the metal of your car and there are so many more bikes to cars that I'm not sure if any of these lights would have the induction loops."

"Fine, fine." Script looked around for something we could mess with. We passed two cars that were still hackable because a patch was missing. They gasped and came to a halt in front of a club. The music poured out onto the street anytime someone came in or out. "If you change the song that's playing in front of all those people, there's no way I'll believe it's fake."

"Me? Why don't you?"

"Okay." Script shrugged and pulled the door open.

"No, wait!" I followed after, giving a quick awkward bow to a bouncer. And maybe one too many *sorry's* as I cut in front of someone to catch back up with Script. "How about we make it interesting and make it a race to see who can hack the music first. More plausible deniability or something that way."

"Dig it."

Behind where the music was coming from were three holographic ladies standing maybe ten feet tall. Their bodies were just wire outlines, but whoever had designed them had made sure they were traditionally sexy. Their exaggerated moves were in time to a DJ who sat in front of the slanted glass that housed the dancers.

This must be how drunk drivers got themselves in trouble. At first I hadn't seen this, but now I almost couldn't take my eyes off the stage. I walked over to the side and caught the sheen of another angled plate of glass.

It was clearly the club's main attraction as it sat in the middle so people could gawk at it from all sides. "I didn't know they scaled this tech up," I said to Script, who was now missing. "Shit, right, the contest."

I sat down in the first open seat I found, wishing we had decided to do this hours ago so I could have figured out beforehand what systems were being used. I reached for a napkin and started ripping it into smaller pieces. A long rectangular piece for the stage and four smaller bits for other speakers around the room. If each were connected separately, there'd be no time to control them all before someone found us out. If they were just wirelessly connected, however, I might be able to bump his signal off and take over. My thoughts drifted towards the hologram system again, and forced myself back to the task at hand.

This wouldn't be the first time I'd pulled this trick. The first had been with a noisy neighbor who didn't mind their volume level in the middle of the night. The fastest route would be to just open my phone and see what Bluetooth devices were in range. The list filled with people's phones, their names first and then what OS they ran.

Remotely accessing Ada was my next bet. With that system's help, I could aircrack the DJ's system. The data it spit back was tough to read on a phone, and if Script had a tablet, I was at a clear disadvantage.

In all fairness, the song currently playing was the perfect hacking soundtrack already. It made me want to leave them alone, so I did, and pursued a new dream by looking for an employee-only area. I found a locked door that looked about right. Something I wasn't meant to touch had to be behind it.

I might not have been as equipped as I used to be, but lockpicks were discrete. Especially ones already made from large paper clips. I had the door open for only a second before I ducked in. An average-looking computer was the room's only light. On the monitor were four images of the dancers, each rotated 90 degrees from the last. On a panel to the side, I saw a list of names and clicked on one. A window opened, previewing what seemed to be demo files.

"This one looks fun," I said, and added it to the queue after the dancers.

"Sumimasen," a voice called from the door, and the security guard now there did not sound pleased.

"This is not the bathroom." I glanced around like I was too drunk to know where I was, let alone read Japanese.

The tight expression shifted into a softer annoyance. "That way."

"Right, right, right," I babbled as I left the room. He didn't seem to know it was meant to be locked. Either way, I headed towards the bathrooms. Script stepped out, blocking my path and held up a tablet. Their fingers hovered up for dramatic effect before they hit a large next button.

I knew what was coming before their finger lifted. The song suddenly faded into a new one, leaving the crowd to shrug it off as an accident more than anything else.

"You cheated! I couldn't read the hash well enough from my phone." I glanced behind me, and the guard was no longer watching so I dropped the ruse of going somewhere.

"What's that?" Script asked and hit next again, raising everyone's suspicions higher. It was like they'd punched me in the chest with the threat of being caught again. "Truth is neither could I, so I paid someone to let me use their tablet."

"Look." I pointed to the stage. The women dimmed and holographic jellyfish floated up in their place. The natural orange-red tint and translucency of the creature worked even better for the set up. Tentacles reached for the musician like a monster only barely held off by the music being played.

"That's so fucking cool!" Script turned back to scoop my hands in theirs. "What else can we change it to?"

If I looked dazed, Script didn't seem to notice. "Uh, I wanted to find a Godzilla-type monster, but I was able to queue only the jelly before the guard found me."

"Oh, you mean that chap?" Script pointed over my shoulder, and I glanced to find the original guard with an overly beefed-up buddy.

"We need to go." I didn't ask, pulling them along to make a break for it.

"Aw, at least let me change the song again!" The tablet was still in their hand, so I was glad I insisted before we both ended up in jail for messing with a fancy-as-fuck PA system. No clear exit was marked but I made the first sharp turn I could find, which was into a VIP section. I pulled us towards the back wall, hoping we'd just blend in with those who were actually meant to be up here.

Script fell into the first open couch that didn't seem reversed for the night. "Wantta know what song I would have changed it to just then?"

"What?"

"'Better Hide, Better Run.'"

"You're an ass." I laughed and decided we were safe enough that I could also relax into the booth.

The club-goers fell back into sync with the DJ, and a song later the ladies came back, to my disappointment. I missed the jellyfish, but the other sea life would have been interesting. How many people can say they had an underwater rave with giant sea creatures?

"Hey, you're still *with* Sonia, right?"

Maybe I was more drunk than I thought because that seemed to come out of nowhere. "Yes?"

Script nodded, and leaned forward as if instinctively reaching for a drink; when they didn't find one, they opted for the tablet there instead. When they moved out the shadow they'd been sitting in, their face was flushed.

My hand rubbed over my chest. I felt uncomfortably warm all of a sudden. "I—didn't know you were into my type?" What was I even asking? I wasn't even sure if I had understood the start of this conversation, making Script's lost expression feel fair.

Script snorted like I'd said something stupid. "I know this is going to sound directly related, but it's only sort of. Would it be weird if I asked your gender?"

"I don't know."

"I get it, it's cool. Sorry if I made you uncomfortable."

"No, I mean sometimes I'm not sure." Now I wished we had ordered drinks so I could have swallowed down the rush of words. "Sometimes I just don't think I get it. Like I'll feel male, I guess, then sometimes forget it's supposed to be a thing at all. I don't think I feel things the same as others.'"

"Whatever your answer, getting drunk and forgetting your own gender is a good type." Script leaned forward again to change the song, but spotted the bouncers again. They held down an icon and deleted an app. "We should really run for it this time."

One really should never run after drinking for the obvious reasons of coordination, and that jumping up and over multicolored trash bins requires precision. The last one toppled over and I slid to the ground. Script tipped up after me as I pushed myself up and kept going until we were both down the street far enough that we could barely see the club.

It didn't seem like anyone had followed us outside the club itself, which made sense, but I refused to outright stop until I knew for sure. A cop car drove by and I tensed so hard, I thought my knees were going to give out. It casually just drove through when the light turned green. "Oh god, that was something."

"Yeah." Script leaned over on their knees. "I also really need water."

"There's a machine on the way back to the house."

They nodded, and I thought they might lose their stomach before standing up again. We walked the rest of the way back slowly and while sharing a bottle we'd brought along the way.

We lost the morning to sleep and fending off hangovers, but by noon Script had to head out to catch their plane. The sober light of day made last night seem even more ridiculous. We got ready separately but without real issue, despite the one bathroom.

Script stood at my door, backpack on and waiting for their ride to the airport to come. I had offered to take the train with them, but they elected to splurge on a taxi for some quiet time. "Hey Scott," they said, voice lifting nervously by the end.

"Yeah?"

"I'm sorry if things got weird at all last night. Sometimes I get a little... direct when drinking, and I definitely shouldn't have nearly gotten you in trouble."

"It's alright. I enjoyed the company. It's nice having you around for more than just firefights."

They laughed before chewing on their bottom lip. "You know about what you said last night? There's a word for that. It's close to genderflux."

Without even knowing the full meaning, I knew liked it. "I didn't know that was one of the options."

"Everything's an option. There are endless words. Remember that, okay?"

"New Wi-Fi detected," Ada reported as a trio of tiny drones sprang to life, jumping into the air with a mechanical whirl.

Panic leaked in every sense. I was trying to remember that not every moment had to be a *Thing.* But that definitely wasn't a good sign. She was only meant to send out drones if the signal was close enough to basically be on top of us.

Being upstairs at the time meant there was a little protection, since the only way you could get up here was the stairs, but it wasn't like the paper that made up these doors had a lock. I could run across to the bedroom—*just breathe first.*

I pulled up the drones' feeds, and saw our trash? Behind our bins there was a lump like a misplaced bag. The shape moved as the other bin's lid lifted. The corner of the screen showed the signal strength and an SSID. The drones were inside and hadn't been spotted yet, as the guy's hotspot overlapped into the house.

There was something undignified about digging in trash that ended my fear of him. Rather than hide, I headed downstairs to confront him. One of the drones followed me out like an overeager pet. "You are on private property."

Their clothes looked crumpled but not ruined by the trash, as if he were still protecting an old suit. If someone *needed* something out of my trash, I wouldn't have cared, but that didn't seem to be the case here. "You're a PI, aren't you? Bet this wasn't how you expected to spend your trip."

The deer-in-the-headlights shock wore off fast and settled on nervous embarrassment. "Might have paid for my trip, so…"

"Hey, I have a question for you." I scooped the lid back on and the man pulled his hands back so they didn't get pinched. With an elbow leaning on the top, I asked, "Do you know if Japan has stand-your-ground laws? Because in America, they allow you to get away with murder."

The man paled to a whiter shade of white. "I, uh, I don't know."

I nodded along. "Want to find out? Because I have a *really* good lawyer."

He looked at the ground, as if there'd be a clear line that divided everything neatly up. Without one, he nervously laughed. "That's okay. Have a good afternoon, Mr. Gris."

I wordlessly watched him go because I couldn't think of anything to reply that didn't make me feel childish, or that would make me look better when I forwarded the video of this to my lawyer.

I doubted anything would come of it, but at least she'd be informed and the guy's face would be in a file somewhere. Maybe I should get a cat, so if anyone else wants our trash, it will be mixed with used litter. Sonia would come back in three days, which meant just three days until my sense of normalcy came back as well.

Despite every system reporting all clear, I couldn't shake the feeling of someone hiring people out to follow what I do. After hours of paranoia, I just gave up and headed out. Depending on who and why someone was trying to track me would change how easily I could lose them. My main concern was a state agency. Random assholes I could deal with myself. The cops showing up at my house with a warrant, I could not.

Thankfully, checking into a hotel discreetly was easy enough. I didn't know if it was because love hotels had set a standard, or if it was because the receptionist was overly kind. The security here was worse than staying at home, but my location was hidden within one of many rooms under a fake name. It would also force someone to decide which they wanted more: something in my house, or me.

I slept shallowly, only half-realizing I had been when a door closing jolted me awake. I sat up before I knew it and my head spun for the combination. Nothing in here except my rough breathing. The sound must've been from the hallway. *Why is trying to live an average life so much harder than fighting?*

This idea brought some safety, but also made every shadow a monster. Maybe the only way I could prove to myself that the world would be okay was to walk in it. I pulled up my hood and walked around the hotel to see what they had to offer before hitting the streets, traveling aimlessly for a few hours before pausing.

Spray-painted over a concrete street divider were kanji characters. I pulled out my phone using my camera and finger to highlight the words. By the end there was a tiny message that translated to *I understand nothing at all.* I didn't know who had come before, but I definitely felt a kinship with them right now.

I stared at the message for another moment before I decided I had to do something besides run scared. Seiji was the only one whose judgement I didn't fear making a request from, and I sent a text off. *Hey, do you have anything I can work on tonight?*

I had been hanging out in a park for a half hour before a message came back. *You're not going to like it.*

I didn't like any of today, why stop now?

Take out your trash, the next message read.

"What?" My own voice broke the evening's silence. Did Seiji know about that PI? The app had lagged and soon context came in the form of four photos. One was a translated article detailing who they thought killed the UltSyn worker on the street. No name was listed, just general details that were based off the photos. The last was what I assumed was a map of his location currently.

Japan was fairly safe. Maybe it was because there was no lobbying group fear mongering everyone to be packing heat to defend themselves with. But that didn't mean there still weren't places that sold to that fear.

A gun might have made this whole thing easier, but in truth, I didn't like them much anymore. They gave complicated things an illusion of simplicity. It felt too obvious to ask a store clerk for something else behind glass, so I opted for a DIY solution.

When I checked out, all I had was a disposable camera, PVC coupling, tape, and glue. The first item felt believable and the cashier didn't blink at the rest. Even with double-checking the coupling against my ring size.

I walked down the street and set my bag down on a table outside a closed restaurant. The camera came apart without much hassle, and the device I ended up with was solid black, like a bulky ace ring with two metal bolts that would arc electricity. The camera's battery would only power the taser for one good hit, but making it rechargeable would take time I did not have right now.

The rest of the camera's flash mechanics were dumped into my pocket as I slid the ring onto my finger. It sat snugly next to the bright white scar where someone had cut the last time I had done anything remotely vigilante-like. Maybe that should have been a warning, but the symmetry was oddly comforting.

I didn't know what Sonia would have done or even wanted if she had been here. Since she wasn't, I only knew of my way to get something done. As I headed across town, I realized the hypocrisy of what I was planning on doing. Even if I was still making up 90% of the details as I was going. But figured that all action was contextual and that reactionary violence was where the glorification of all action heroes came from in the first place. Plus, it wasn't like I was gonna kill the dude.

If he had been at home, I might have been screwed if I wanted this to be only a one-night thing. But the address Seiji gave me was a bar. With my hands stuffed in my pockets, I headed inside.

I wish I could say I used deduction to figure out what type of man he was by his haircut, but in reality he aggressively stood out. Would have even been my guess if no photos were sent. He was swinging his arms around, and he had broad shoulders that made him look like Gaston. He also treated women about the same. Within the first minute of my watching, he goosed the poor waitress who was just trying to walk by. Her expression tightly held back her feelings on the matter. His laugh made it doubtful that that was the first time she had been bothered tonight.

The phrase "seeing red" always seemed to imply that everything turned that color. When it happened to me, the only color that remained was the red details on clothes. *Maybe I would kill him…*

My trigger-happiness shattered when he spoke. I didn't even process the words over the weight of his accent. American, like mine. That's what Seiji meant by *my trash*.

"You need to leave," I said, stepping up behind the man. He swiveled around in his chair, and when he saw my face, he leaned back. It didn't seem as if he recognized me as much as he was just surprised to be called out at all.

"What do you want to do?" He chuckled and reached back for his drink. "Fight about it?"

My fist tightened in my pocket. "Yeah, I fucking do."

He got up from his seat, and I didn't move. "Let's go outside. There's no room here."

"Alright, fine." He pinched his shirt as if used to something more formal. "Get your ass kicked into the asphalt if you want."

I did my best to say nothing else that might be deemed colorful and therefore memorable as I headed outside and waited for him long enough to chug the rest of his drink. "Is that your bike?" I asked, pointing to a Harley-Davidson parked in the tiny lot. It was obnoxious, and likely extremely expensive to get imported.

He glanced over, torn between boasting and just decking me. "Yeah, maybe I'll run you over with it after this."

"Yeah, okay," I scoffed and put my fists up.

He swung first. I ducked to the side instead of trying to punch back. If I beat him up, he'd still be in town to harass or even outright kill another person. His second swing went lower than I expected. Pain erupted up my side and across my ribs as I stumbled away.

When he stepped over, I went straight for his neck where the taser would hurt most. He seized up before dropping away from me. Wasting no time, I pulled him back up enough to choke him out.

His strength returned to thrash around. I kept up the pressure and he passed out without landing a second hit. Unceremoniously, I just dropped him on the ground.

Maybe I should have held on, but I froze with the sudden realization of what I just did. After whispering what had to be my hundredth cuss, I started searching his pockets for the keys. The whole time, I thought he'd wake up, but I found a Harley-Davidson keychain first. Not knowing what else to do, I pulled the guy up and slung him over the back of the motorcycle. It looked like a great way for him to fall off, and there wasn't even a helmet to give him.

No one had come out of the bar *yet,* and I wasn't risking that they'd come outside, so I jumped on the front of the motorcycle and hoped the handlebar placement wouldn't throw me off. I obeyed the speed limits; if anything, I went under, because I was afraid his weight would cause a crash.

At the first red light, I came to a full stop and then straight up called Seiji. "Where's the dump?" I asked the second the phone connected.

After an utterance or two and what I thought was his own cuss, he answered. "There's someone I know at the Port Diamond Point who can help you. Drive him there."

"How far is that?"

"Uh, twenty minutes? Could be shorter, but you should avoid the toll."

"If I don't survive, tell my wife I said hello," I joked.

Seiji paused. "You aren't married?"

Damn it, if Sonia were here she would have gotten that. "Just call me in fifteen to tell me who I'm looking for." I hung up because paying attention to the road, phone, and the passed-out violent lecher was too much.

I don't know what god was watching over me, but when that phone rang again fifteen minutes later, I'd happily pay tribute to whoever claimed responsibility. "Is he still out cold?" Seiji asked when he called again.

"For now." I slowed to a near stop to take a turn before trying to make up some speed on a straightaway. "Where am I going?"

"Drive out to this… island past ours until you see cargo containers. There'll be a guy with blue hair waiting for you."

"How do you know him?" Maybe this was a trap. Maybe Seiji wanted us both out of their city. Each meter closer raised my blood pressure.

"He's a tattoo artist."

"What?" That didn't sound like the right answer or someone trying to trick me. It was oddly candid.

"He works at the docks part time, and can get that asshole to Germany or wherever tonight's shipment is going," Seiji explained. "Real paranoid about state surveillance, which means he's always willing to smuggle stuff for whoever is willing to keep the cameras off his back."

I pulled to a stop and didn't see the blue haired guy yet. "Which is your doing?"

"No." I expected Seiji to follow up with *Neko obviously, Scott. Come on.* But the word I heard was very different. "Yakuza."

I thought back to the graffiti. *"Zen zen Wakarimasen."*

Seiji laughed, leaving me with no idea if this was an area the mob ran or if he thought it was just funny. "Welcome to Japan, Scott-san."

A short girl named after a cat was sitting on another hotel room's TV stand. She was currently flipping me off as I sat in the corner of the room. *Brother.*

Funny, I signed back.

UltSyn, Neko spelled out with a recognizable blur. *Made everyone learn an official, yet bastardized, ASL. But some things don't translate or people refuse to change what they are used to.*

"I even learned it to help her practice," Seiji said, and signed from his spot on the floor. "But it seems their attempts at a universal sign language have been halted. Did my contact make you promise anything?"

Hesitation slowed my reply. "How did you know?"

He always demands something, Neko said.

"May have promised to get a tattoo."

Neko grinned. *Please tell me he randomly brought that up.*

What? My tight expression was 95% of the sign, I swear. Maybe the idea of me awkwardly asking a stranger to kidnap a different stranger with the bribe of adding to his portfolio was just too funny. *No, he more demanded it.*

"Dude's a riot," Seiji added.

I just shook my head at the whole thing. An improbability strung together with another like threaded candy. That's what everything was.

Can I call you my trash collector? Neko asked. Eyes bright, like she had a list waiting.

One-time thing. I leaned all the way back in my chair and no one called out what I think we all knew would end up being a lie. When they left, I had access to their private chat room. I expected just their handles, not a multi-channeled encrypted space. I even stayed up until morning deciding if I wanted to be obviously me, or if I wanted an under-the-radar username.

All I could truly focus on was how it's a dangerous thing to pretend to be someone you're not. I wondered if that's why I was here in this hotel while Sonia was off dealing with UltSyn matters. If Emmett Harris could have been anything besides a predator, he wouldn't wake up in a storage container headed somewhere that was promised to be a safe distance away. I learned his name afterwards. Hadn't even asked for it beforehand. And maybe didn't even care what happened to him.

It wasn't the silence that sent my thoughts spiraling, it was the stillness. I used to think the world was predictable. Big mistake. You had to make a choice every second and every day. While everyone else did the exact same thing. Existing was proving harder without a guiding star. I wanted Sonia to be that, but it's a lot to put on a person who could save themself. All I knew for sure is I wanted to go home.

Ada hadn't reported anything besides a false alarm caused by wind anyways. I stepped back into my house feeling nostalgic for moments I hadn't had yet. A couple hours later, the door opened to one of those times.

"Surprise!" Sonia said, juggling her bags. "I'm back early." She leaned in to give me a peck of a kiss before putting her bags down.

"Certainly is." I was amazed at how much just being in the same room together meant to me. As she unpacked, I kept her company and opened the group chat to casually figure out who was who. "Make any new friends while you were away?"

"Ha, no." She made a small pile of dirty stuff. "How about you?"

"Does further befriending the two people we know already count?" The user Deaf Cat For Cutie was definitely Neko. My eyes caught the English every single time she posted. That left another eleven names, and I saw no wordplay that hinted at Seiji. That, or the pun was something I missed in translation.

This chat was only offered after I'd helped forcefully remove someone from the country, so I assumed everyone here was trusted with shady things. That fact dampened my urge to find them all online. I settled on SxS. It was a flash memory type that wasn't often seen, but it also worked as a stand-in for Scott and Sonia, or if I wanted to throw people off, an off-road vehicle. The name got a choir of greetings but no direct mention that they knew who I was.

A quick favor for Sonia caused an avalanche of messages to build up. So many messages that the app's sound lagged. I scrolled through most of it to find where I was mentioned and it just read, *You're against homelessness, right?*

There was no way they expected me to somehow fix that. Maybe they just wanted me to see the plights of an area I was trying to call home? There was certainly enough of it around here to be an issue.

"It's so quiet here. I dunno how you do it," Sonia said, and turned on the TV. Since it was just for the sound, she left it on whatever channel it had been on before it was turned off. I shrugged since things had actually been louder since she had returned. The zip of her bag, steps that weren't mine, they all just stood out more than background noise.

The news talked about something without a real sense of urgency until a breaking news banner appeared. The bottom chyron read, *Another Standoff in Nishinari-ku Ward*, or something similar. A reporter spoke to a group standing to the side, and I had my phone listen to the audio so it could spit out a halfway decent translation. The audio feeds on top of each other made it hard to fully understand, but the heart of the matter was that day laborers were upset with the police.

"They need to be put to work," Sonia said.

"They are trying to work, they need to be left alone." Plenty of them ended up without a place to go to back to at night, since day-to-day pay offered no stability. Criminalizing being homeless instead of targeting the systems that caused the problem in the first place would change nothing except appearances.

"Noble, but you can't just opt out of paying rent."

I did. Obviously not right now, but when I'd met Sonia I had been squatting. I knew what she meant and arguing about it wasn't going to change what I was seeing on TV, so I held back and watched. The ad breaks in the middle of a civil standoff made the network seem like it didn't care. "Why are we even sitting here? It's only like an hour away."

"What can we do besides get in the way?"

"You wanted to help former workers. If day laborers settled in that area, why wouldn't displaced UltSyn workers? We already found two. Find out who they are before the police do."

"You don't think—" Sonia didn't finish that thought. I didn't know what she was going to say. That the police would beat them, or target them specifically for upsetting the balance, or something else entirely. Any horror felt possible.

Everyone was masked up when we got there. Most with the paper-thin sort you see on the train. But enough had cloth masks, and a few even more legit ones around their face. That was enough to trigger the police to preemptively wear gas masks.

By only watching on TV, you'd never know most of the so-called rioters were elderly. I hadn't seen a kid yet, and even we verged on the young side. People self-divided into three groups. The police, onlookers, and the protesters, which had grown to far more than just the workers themselves.

The police didn't have riot shields yet for whatever it was worth, but the tension in the air was heavy, as if ready to crack open into chaos. From the best I could tell, most protestors were traveling to a police station, which caused more officers to step out to defend it as if it was their very own temple.

"You're right." I glanced over to Sonia standing next to me. "I don't know what we can do here."

"We are tough. There must be something."

With a foot off the sidewalk, I turned towards the protesters, who as a group were trying to keep moving despite the cops' best efforts to box them in. Money had it that if anyone stayed still for too long or became too separated from each other, arrests could be made. "I'm going to make some L.A.W."

I waited to see if Sonia was going to join me. She didn't look directly at me or seem focused on much of anything. If I was hesitating at the edge of the group, Sonia took it to the whole next level. I hadn't realized she'd brought back from

China a sense of doubt in my ideas. "That's liquid antacid and water, right?" she finally replied.

"Specific hydroxide ones, yeah."

"If it comes to pepper spray…" She sighed heavily. "Better safe than sorry, I guess."

"What do you want me to do?" I sighed. Companies live and die, but protests against the police were as old as their existence.

"I don't know. This doesn't feel like the right way."

That seemed unfair; risking your skull being cracked open on the road was as brave as anything I did. Sure, not everyone here would go that far, but as I spotted someone pull a glass bottle from a recycle bin, I knew enough were willing.

She shook her head. "Whatever, it's up to you."

That answer wasn't a gift, it was a burden.

<chapter fifteen>
<! -- Sonia -->

When we got home, I told Scott what I wanted to do. It started with knowing how many people like me are here. We were cuddled on the couch when I spoke to the air in front of me rather than him directly. People had power in numbers, but only if organized. That's what Terry proved with his non-profit. Scott was right about everything coming down to power. And I needed some.

"Hand me my phone." That's all Scott said before he sat up and got to work. The idea went nowhere for a week, and regret over asking started eating its way up. But it turns out the police were working on the same curiosity. Get a copy of that single database and one didn't need to break into any police systems.

Scott's list of people with UltSyn architecture was already up to five. Which was less than the official list by either his expertise or willful design. I asked Scott how he knew his list was correct, and he mentioned painstakingly trying to match photos taken of the protest against public social media accounts to find candidates that were most likely.

He didn't tell me how he got a copy of the law enforcement list, and I didn't ask, figuring it only fair since I was working on a project I hadn't told him about either. Harry had promised to tell me more when he came to Japan. It was a trip I had waited for while still on my own trip.

It almost felt like an affair with my past life. I went places in town I hadn't ever needed before just for this meetup, and without fanfare declared what I wanted once again. "You said you'd prove it when you got back to Japan."

"You cut to the chase, don't you?" Harry was window shopping through a long stretch of underground subway. Above us was just a thick sheet of concrete. The paths were designed to be standard size, but it still felt otherworldly. For someone whose finances should be in ruins, these stores weren't of the cheap souvenir sort. "I can respect that," he said and pulled an envelope out from his coat pocket.

The things inside hadn't always been there. Most evidently by a photo that stuck out past the seal. It was of two men; one had his arm swung over what looked like a much younger Harry's shoulders. They both looked excited about something. "Is this you?"

"Yeah, and your father and I right before a launch party. We didn't see the bad back then. Guess that's what happens when your job is to work on making the UI pretty."

I silently stared at the photo. This had to be from before I was born since his outfit and hair were a time capsule of a long abandoned style. My father and I weren't identical by any means, but I really could see similarities in the cheeks and how our eyes were.

"His name was Kristopher by the way. With a K."

I repeated the name in my head, but I didn't need any tech to know I'd remember it forever. I put the photo back and now the name on the envelope made sense. It was from him. I foolishly hoped they'd be a *In case I died* letter, but instead I found a group Christmas letter. "Eve and I are expecting," I said out loud without really meaning to. I looked up to Harry, wide-eyed, and he seemed to nod at my unspoken question.

"You," he said softly before going on. "We were working on different projects by this point, but I actually saw you once before. You must have been only three feet tall back then."

I opened the envelope further but there was nothing more. "I, uh, didn't even know he worked for UltSyn."

"Him and your grandfather. He was very proud of that fact and would joke that it was like the old days when a family could do the same job for generations. I'd reminded him that he didn't do that same job, but he claimed it was close enough." Harry laughed.

"My…" Words were getting hard, but I didn't know if he knew how to sign so I pushed through. "My grandfather?" First my father, then the name of my mother, just how much family would I get back?

"Stuff of legends. Well, in the right circles. There weren't photos of him on the walls or anything. He was friends with the founder. I figured it was something casual, like my friendship with Kristopher. This brings me to why I wanted to talk to you more in person. I want you to help me with something."

"Me? Why not ask Scott or Terry?" I pulled the letter and photo closer to my chest, and scolded myself for being so transparent about wanting to keep them.

"Please, Terry would stop for every lost puppy on the road," Harry said. "I don't know what Scott does these days, but I know I'm able to stay focused on this. Like I'm sure you'd be, too." He folded his arms across his chest, and glanced around before leaning in. "I bought up UltSyn's stock as it nosedived. It's worth nothing right now, but you could shape it in *your* image."

"You'd just give it to me?"

"The job of leading UltSyn away from the direction that shit on people like you?" He broke into a smile. "Who better? Maybe someday I can give something that was once broken to my own daughter."

"Can I keep these?" I looked down at the envelope again.

"Of course. I wish I'd saved more, I just didn't know they'd be important again."

"I need to think about it." I told myself to put everything away, but a part of me believed that if I secured them anywhere besides in my hand, they'd vanish like they'd never existed in the first place.

He chuckled. "Sorry, you just sounded like him. Your family isn't known for being impulsive."

"What were they known for?"

"Being thoughtful."

I came home to a completed list of suspected former UltSyn workers who had been at the protest. Contacting them might yield more who didn't show up that day. It wasn't fair that they couldn't bank on something as fickle as notoriety like I could, but soon I might be able to fix all that.

After today, I had every answer I'd ever wanted at my fingertips. "Is this what it's like to be a god?"

Scott glanced over from the screens connected to his laptop. I couldn't read the expression because the data was too beautiful to look away from. Laid out like a work of art. "Wouldn't know."

"Because if it's omnipotence... I'm starting to understand."

"Uh?" His voice hung in the air as if waiting for me to go on. When I didn't, he shook his head. "Hey, I need a break. I know it's a silly idea, but do you want to have a picnic of sorts on our balcony? It seems like a good way to get away without actually having to go anywhere."

The photo turned to lead in my coat pocket. "I can't," I blurted. Having to wait any longer to see what was inside again sounded like a nightmare, and I wasn't ready to share.

"Oh, okay. Maybe later."

It must've been around three in the morning. Scott was sleeping next to me, while I was sitting up in bed for at least an hour. If not more. Did I even know if Harry was telling the truth? Scott's breathing changed with a whine, and turned over. I watched until the tossing settled down, thinking that I should wake him up and tell him about my father. Was it fair to burden him with my family when he couldn't see his own either?

Who could I talk to about this? Neko and Seiji were our friends, right? I sat up on my knees so I could reach over and grab his phone from the nightstand. I unlocked his phone and messaged the chat to see if anyone could help.

Can any of you check the validity of some personal things I found? - Sonia, I typed. The unsent message stared at me for a moment. Maybe I should just delete this and figure it out myself. But, I wanted help. Maybe *needed* someone who wouldn't be biased about the answer.

After hitting send, my head debated other minor details, like if I should put the phone back or if I'd just have to reach over for it again. My thoughts spiraled with half a dozen possibilities until I just settled down in bed with it close.

The chime that followed made my heart soar. *Please be related to my message, please be related to my message.* The app loaded slowly, then finally—

Sure, send it over.

The tightness around my chest cleared. I didn't even know who had offered, but it didn't feel like it mattered, since someone had been there when I needed it. *Thanks, I'll PM you.*

The permission somehow made it okay for me to add the username on my phone after downloading the app for myself. They made me prove it was me this time by using Scott's phone to confirm it.

Another message came right way. *Us girls can never be too safe, right? =^..^=*

This definitely had to be Neko. I was trying to think of cute ASCII art to send back but didn't think of any before finally falling asleep, hoping I'd know the truth by morning. The next day, every time Scott's phone went off, I wished it was mine. By afternoon it finally was.

One chime. *Looks real to me.*

A second. *Only way I can check further is if you bring the originals.*

Dizziness washed over me, and instead of holding myself up, I just allowed myself to carefully half-fall, half-sit, on the bottom stair.

"Are you okay?"

"Yes."

Scott hovered above me for a moment. Maybe my answer had come too fast for him to believe it. "You can say no, it won't mean you are falling apart." That was the answer of someone who mentally answered no more times than they deserved.

"Thank you. I really am fine, just been a lot lately. Maybe I just need some water."

"I understand. I'll go get you some." He carefully stepped around me and into the kitchen.

I didn't realize the ways Scott could fall apart until I found him the later that week just frozen on the floor. In front of him were seven manila folders. They had no labels, so I picked one up. They were of the dead UltSyn workers, but not those who'd signed up for help. The dates and details confirmed that they'd served as our guards while Scott had been searching for his sister. "Why do you have these?"

"I got so tired looking for people who didn't ask to be found before realizing I didn't even know who I had killed beyond the names." Scott gestured to the collection still in my hand. "That guy abused his wife like four times, so fuck him. But this guy…" He just stared at another file before his hand reached out to touch it. "By all reasonable accounts he was just doing his job. Nothing shows he knew the harm he was doing."

I tossed the papers down and sat on the floor with Scott. "They say nice people make the best bad guys. They will look the other way, ignore all the signs, and never make waves, so civility can continue. Nice is proper, but nice isn't always good or kind."

He said nothing, and I thought he'd ignored me until he rested his head on my shoulder. "The answer to the trolley problem is that it should be your own life. You should be the one paying the price. The morally pure choice would harm no one but myself."

"Scott," I breathed out. "Please, don't do this to yourself."

"You see," he continued as if I had said nothing at all. "That's how we trick ourselves into solving it. Someone we care about stands on one side, and suddenly the answer is so clear."

"Look at me."

Reluctantly, he lifted his head to do so.

"Can you honestly tell me there was a single time where you could have protected me or your sister by bleeding just a little more?"

"I did everything I could." His response had come slow and I didn't realize that he was stalling until he finished. "Guess we should get back to real work."

I checked the time and had to agree. Protecting UltSyn itself was never either of our goals, but a legacy was possible. Scott's actions had opened so many opportunities for me, and if he had to live with guilt, maybe I could use it for something. I used a grocery run as an excuse to call Harry back.

He picked up on the second ring. "Hey you, have you thought about things more?"

"Yeah actually, but I have a few more questions first."

"I have..." Harry's voice stretched out as if checking something. "Four hours till my flight. Did you want to meet up?"

"That's okay, I'm more thinking out loud."

"Alright."

I adjusted the bags in my one hand, thinking I should have brought along headphones. "If I agree, what would your job be?"

"I'm a UI designer, so unless you need help with any of those programs, I'll likely just focus on doing admin and PR stuff that you don't want to tackle or need help with."

"And I don't have to leave Japan?"

"Not unless you wanted to." His laugh sounded higher over the phone than it did in person. "I have an office here, but half the time I'm on the road. Doesn't mean you have to be. That's the perk of things being international already."

"I'm in."

"Really? That's wonderful. I'll cancel my flight so we can start on this right away. Working with your father was among the best years of my career. Please forgive me if I'm a little excited."

The crosswalk signal in front of me was ticking down the last seconds and it didn't seem wise to run across with my hands full. "What's the first thing we have to do?"

"I can set up a press conference. All you need to do is decide what you want to say. Ideally what you hope for in the future."

"What if I don't know what I want to hope for?"

"Be vague. Follow-through is less important here than you might think."

I laughed, and the streetlight turned green again as if it also approved. "I'll get working on it."

"Talk to you then."

"Great, call you back when I have more details."

I hung up and carefully wiggled my phone back in my pants pocket. Home didn't seem so far away anymore. When I started putting the groceries away, the whole world even seemed normal. I'd secured a job and was well on my way to putting groceries away. Maybe the whole world could stay normal long enough for me to enjoy it a moment.

Days spent chasing conventionalism cause warning signs to be overlooked—assumed to be okay as our gaze falls elsewhere. It had been awfully still in our house, and I looked up from the tablet I was typing half-formed ideas into. Scott touched a blind and caused the light in the room to rise and strobe softly as gravity fought against his movement.

"What are you doing?" I asked.

He shook his head at my question. I watched for a moment longer, his legs stretching off the small cushion he sat on, but he looked anything but content.

"You asked me weeks ago, but I never asked what you wanted."

Scott's fingers wove between the rays of dust floating in the air. Their existence flicked in and out before the blind finally came to a stop. "To live in the light." He pulled back, and looked towards me but didn't look focused. "I feel like these past few weeks I've been nothing more than a tool. I thought I wouldn't care if it protected people. But being used for a good cause still feels like being used. And I don't want to fight like this or with people who aren't my comrades. Maybe I'd rather be alone."

At the last word, his eyes fully found mine. The intensity threw me off. He was sure of himself, somehow even now. The guilt of trying to simply be seemed piled on top of the weight of once having action in every second.

"When everything about us is politicized. Simply existing is fighting back."

He inhaled sharply. My comment felt like a seed. One day it might bloom into something helpful, but not without time.

"Stand up."

"Why?"

I stood up, moved to the middle point of the room. He got up and mirrored me, until I put a hand on his chest. "It's all a matter of heart. You have to ask yourself. Where is yours?"

"Still with you," he whispered and took my free hand in his.

"I've seen heart in everything you touch. I don't want you to lose that. Don't say yes to everything if it won't make you happy." There was a beat of silence. "And, I'm sorry if I've seemed distant. That's what I've been trying to do myself."

"Has it been working?"

"Yeah, actually."

"Then that's what matters." There was something sad about his expression, like maybe he wished he was part of it. Like I often wished to be a more active part of the chat room instead of just witnessing it afterward.

"Just focus on whatever you've already promised and then figure it out from there." He seemed unsure, but agreeable enough. "Hey, maybe we should have that picnic now."

A raw joy broke through his expression and his shoulders relaxed at the suggestion alone. "If you get us snacks, I can pull our bedding out there."

I didn't know if it was a proper thing to do here, since I was sure our feet would end up near black from the dust, but it sounded perfect. "It's a date."

<chapter sixteen>
<! – Scott -->

I figured out which username was the dock worker because I dug around enough to find posts showing off a new tattoo. His face was blocked out with an emoji, but it was enough to still tell who it was. Talking to him casually online before meeting up in person again made his question only slightly less intimidating. I adjusted an earpiece that was meant to translate his voice in real time. Maybe it was just being asked the question behind a bunch of houses that raised an alarm. "My what now?"

"Your blood type."

Guess this thing was working. "If you have to give me a blood transfusion for a tattoo, I'm going to break my promise."

Good job, you didn't even make it inside before confusing him, Haru, Neko signed before knocking on the back door. The door opened up without a person on the flip side.

"It's so I can know your personality type," he said, then proceeded to explain the system at length to me. A blood was sensitive and fastidious, B for irresponsible doers, AB people were controlled but critical, and Type O was saved for optimists who verged on carelessness. A secure metal door slid open and Haru continued even as we walked in. "You strike me as AB, being the ambitious sort. I'm B." He pulled his sleeve up to show a large tattoo of a blood bag high on his arm. It sported a large letter in the middle of it and a red cord that ran down his arm before looping back up.

"That must come in handy if you're in an accident."

"It has," Seiji said, likely before my sentence even translated to Haru's earpiece. He came down a set of small stairs in a black tank top and boxer briefs. Staring hadn't been my intent, but it was impossible to not follow the tattoo running down one leg. The thigh had four solid black blocks that curved before dipping past the knee in thin lines, as if pouring into an equally large patch of dark honeycombs, before turning into lines at the ankle and stopping at the toes. God, how many hours did that piece take?

A sharp poke in my side caused me to twitch, and I snapped out of it to see Neko with a pencil in her hand. "Feeling chicken?" She didn't even wait for an answer, just smirked before walking off.

"Are you allowed to be pantsless in a tattoo parlor?" I asked. There were two identical workstations set up right in front, then a small open waiting room where a couch sat. Which was where this place stopped looking like a hidden away business and started looking like an apartment.

"In my parlor he can be," Haru said, and plopped into a spinning chair.

"You mean I let you tattoo people in my house," Seiji teased back. He spoke in Japanese and I had gotten so used to his voice that the pre-programmed voice translation that followed sounded wrong.

"Sit, sit," Haru called.

"I told Sonia I'd be back today, and I've never had a tattoo before," I babbled, but followed instructions.

"I always go gentle on first timers." Haru was busy preparing the tattoo gun and actually offered very little reassurance. I couldn't even tell if he was being suggestive or if his true tone had been edited out.

Neko moved back, opting to lean on the wall in front of me. "Tell her what you doing?"

I started to mouth *no* before a buzzing sound stole my attention. Only after it stopped a second later was I able to finish. "Felt too silly."

She shrugged a shoulder as if she agreed it was.

"Know what you want?" Haru asked.

"Yeah actually, I was thinking about a little heart rate with a semicolon at the end on my wrist."

"Cute," Haru said, and for my own sanity I decided he meant it. I missed talking to him on a platform where he had a habit of overusing reaction images to show intent.

"We should pair it to your actual heart rate," Seiji said, now on our level and wearing tan house slippers that brought an extra softness to such an aggressive tattoo.

"I like that." It was cute, and the twist made it more personal. Haru nodded along as he put his equipment down and started looking for something else. Neko glanced between the lot of us, missing the conversation. Seiji signed, *heart monitor?* and she was up.

She whistled when she found it by a computer in the corner and decided to stay at the station. Seiji went and fetched what turned out to be a fitness tracker that I assumed was hooked up to the computer Neko was at.

I put it on and waited. Silently glancing between the device, Neko and Seiji. Haru impatiently put the tattoo gun down as awkward silence grew, only momentarily interrupted by the sound of Seiji's phone.

"Tell Scott to stop being an anxious fuck," he read off in English.

"What?" I broke into a laugh. "Did she really text you that?"

"No, she texted that your heart rate is elevated. I worded it differently to break the ice." Seiji pulled over a chair from the other workstation. "Ever get burned by a cigarette?"

"No?"

He waved his own question away and pointed down to the tattoo on his leg. "Now, this hurt a lot, but mostly because it took forever. But objectively the scar on my arm hurt a lot more. I got that from a motorcycle mishap. And I wondered why that was so for a long while, until Neko pointed out that I chose one and not the other. You must have some wicked scars, too."

I sat forward in my seat enough to pull off my jacket. A white knot of scar tissue was easy to see when I pulled my shirt sleeve up. "In the moment it didn't hurt much, but everything about it afterward did."

"A tattoo is going to be a reverse of that. It's going to hurt a bit at first but then duller after that. Personally speaking, the vibration is the worst part. You've been shot at, so you got this."

"Maybe I was worried Haru wouldn't tattoo what I wanted, and I'd end up marked as part of a secret society."

"The second half of that is still happening," Haru said a beat after. "Everyone I tattoo is part of my legacy."

Seiji waited for him to finish after being accidentally interrupted. "Haru only pranks foreigners who want hiragana, or that rapist who still thought you'd keep his appointment after the fact."

"All true," Haru agreed, then paused to think for a second. "I also refuse to do The Great Wave without giving it a twist."

The chair felt a lot more comfortable as I leaned back into it. Didn't even realize I was tensing so hard before. "So, what do I do? Just hold still?"

"Yeah."

"If you are gonna pass out or something let us know. But if you can't stand this, I'm going to suspect you are a very elaborate plant trying to earn our trust," Seiji added.

I smiled at the wild realization that I hadn't completely stopped wanting to meet new people after all. The thought that threatened to change everything in an unpredictable way. Would I even know any of them if it hadn't been for every single decision that brought me to Japan?

Neko walked over, and handed a sheet of paper to Haku. *One aesthetically pleasing heart,* she signed. I tried to sit up taller in my chair to sneak a look, but I was sitting at a bad angle as he studied it.

"007 is British, right?" Seiji asked.

My *yes* started out unsure of itself, if not downright confused, before it petered out into a nervous murmur as the tattoo gun pulsed over my wrist. It wasn't a sharp enough pain that I felt like I had to pull away, maybe in part to Seiji's distractions. Instead, I watched the tight ups and down that the scratching vibration laid down on my skin.

"Almost, and…" Haru extended the word, lifting the tattoo gun up for a second before adding the dot of the semicolon. "Done." He wiped it off with rubbing alcohol and let me see before it got wrapped up.

It was red and irritated over the bright blue veins, but really beautiful in simplicity. "Thank you for this."

"A deal's a deal," he said happily. "Easy enough for us both."

I pulled off the fitness tracker and set it by Haru's things.

When I looked up, Neko was staring with a funny little expression that pursed her mouth.

May I ask you a question?

Why not? I signed back.

Are you a grass-eater?

"I... don't think that translates correctly." I looked to Seiji for help.

"She's being improper because she saw a video of your arrival saying you weren't straight." Haru thankfully was cleaning up and not paying attention. "I told her if it's hidden it's a flower, but she's as curious as her namesake."

"I'm just going to look this up to save both of us further awkwardness." I pulled out my phone and twitched at the pain at my wrist before searching for what that meant on the English side of the internet at least. The results left me equally horrified and stunned that despite, different writing systems, both cultures somehow made a similar slang. "I didn't realize plant jokes were international."

"Ah, ours in a pun over how the character for meat can also mean flesh. That's how you get carnivore and herbivore. Or grass-eater. It describes behavior, not an identity, so you can ignore her if you want." He signed so Neko could still understand easily, and in reply she stuck her tongue out.

I chuckled and appreciated the option of avoiding the question if I really did want. I tried to look up what the what

Japanese word for me would be on the English side of the internet but no answer instantly jumped out. Funny how things you fight for in one place were completely different in a different part of the world. As if the Earth was a multiverse unto itself. *Maybe we should stick with non-straight for now,* I signed.

Okay, my non-straight brother, Neko signed. I wasn't sure if she was using brother like same, or if she just really enjoyed having another excuse to flip me off.

"I actually have been wondering about something else." My hands followed the words. "Did you expect me to break the law that night?"

"I was hoping," Seiji said far too casually for its being the most inexcusable thing I had done since in Japan.

Yeah, we won't even tell Sonia. Neko's comment was either mistimed or there was a fissure in the ex-employee ranks I didn't know about. Her movements grew more playful though. *If you really want to prove your worth, you can help me prank my girlfriend.*

She had meant same. I didn't want to make a fuss about it so I just signed, *Sure, I'd love to.*

"I'm out!" Haru interjected. "What? She scares me."

She's sweet like summer rain. Neko now had the flourish of a fountain pen.

"More like a downpour," Haru mumbled, and any further lip reading was promptly ignored.

She's a streamer and I told her a million times her stuff isn't secure, but she doesn't listen or let me fix it. She walked over to the computer and pulled up her girlfriend's page. For a group that had a tattoo artist, knitter, and a pun-loving catgirl, I didn't expect to see a bubbly Japanese girl with an oversized knit sweater dancing along to a game. Siha, who was also in our group chat, also had a decent following.

Did you want something specific? I asked.

If we mess with the game itself, she'll be upset, but anything else is fair game.

I stopped looking at Siha and started looking at the things behind her. It was pretty bare besides two small strings of hanging paper cranes and a floor lamp so that she wasn't dancing in a dark corner. I could see a large white something where the light was. "Is that one of those remote controls for the lights?"

Seiji leaned into my shoulder to get a better look. "Yeah, I use the same type."

"They have a short range. We wouldn't be able to access it from here unless you have an app synced up for it."

"Road trip it is."

I couldn't even remember the last time I'd been in a car. It was once such an important and common thing. Now I was sitting here in the backseat with a tablet in my hand, like a lookout who had to watch if the stream ended early.

Neko parked outside and turned in her seat towards me. *I see that lamp all the time and never even thought of messing with it. Let's ghost-story it.*

Seiji held his light remote out the window to get an extra two feet. "Ready?"

"Ready."

I watched as a light behind her turned off just after she got into the groove of things. It was so casual that Siha just stopped to glance over at it. She darted over to her own remote to turn it back on, but Seiji turned it back on before she had even touched it.

The streamer giggled nervously.

AC unit? Seiji suggested and Neko excitedly pulled out her phone, which did have an app for that.

"It's the curse of the smart house," I mused. The stream halted as Siha tried to figure out what was going on. The chat had decided to spam the ghost emoji between confused comments.

Siha leaned into the screen and muted the stream as she picked up the phone. None of us were sure who she was gonna call until Seiji's phone started to ring. He shot me an amused look as Neko tried to hold back a laugh. When he answered he put it on speakerphone so we both could hear. "Please tell me you're outside with Neko," my earpiece translated.

"I can neither confirm nor deny that we are outside."

"Wait, what's today? Are you with—" Her gasp cut her off and turned to the camera again. *Goodnight with love, chat* she signed before turning off the stream. The chat had an influx of *I love you* hand emojis. Siha rushed outside, nearly bouncing up and down the driveway as we got out of the car.

She gave Neko a hug first before turning to me, as if I were the supernatural being she'd heard about. "It's you!"

"Konbanwa," I said with a bow.

"Konbanwa." Siha smiled. "Uh, how do you do?"

"I'm fine."

She didn't have the tech Haru and I had been using, but almost lagged the same amount over the English. When she remembered what the word meant she smiled brighter. "That's very good."

She's just started learning English so she can teach abroad, Neko signed. She looped her arm through Siha's, high enough that it shouldn't really get in the way of her own signs.

"It's hard enough already, but English really tests the limits of my hearing," Siha added in Japanese. She gestured towards Seiji to come closer and whispered in his ear without pulling away from her girlfriend. The words were too quiet for my earpiece to pick up this time.

He laughed as his cheeks reddened. With a shake of his head he turned back to me. "I assume Neko is going to stay, and someone is going to spot me wearing like nothing if we stay out here. Are you ready to go?"

"Yeah, actually." I looked at my phone. Sonia hadn't messaged me, but should be there by time I got home, especially since we still had to drive all the way back. We said our goodbyes, and on the way to the car I asked what Siha had said.

He seemed to avoid the topic as I sat down in the front seat. "Uh, roughly that you were cute for someone so dangerous."

And there it was. As normal and as playful as my nights could be, the moment could easily be shattered by the reality of how other people saw me. Even if it was meant as a compliment.

***

"There you are," Sonia said as I walked in.

"Sorry I was late. I was talked into a tattoo. It's still kind of raw."

"Really? Oh, ow. I see that." Sonia's fingers were cold even through the covering. "Big long for such a small one."

"Yeah, afterwards Neko introduced me to her girlfriend."

"I like this," Sonia whispered. She gently pushed my fingers down, exposing my wrist further before she kissed right where my hand met my wrist. It felt like the most intimate thing we'd ever done.

I felt shaky as she looked back up, and clearly wasn't hiding it well. "You okay?"

"Yeah, I think I am now."

"I even have a surprise for you tomorrow."

"Really? Is it something I'm going to like?" I bopped her on the nose before I went off to see if we had the right soap for tattoo care.

"I like it," she yelled over. "And I hope you will too."

<chapter seventeen>
<! -- Scott -->

I did not like it. Not one bit. This was a surprise so horrifying I wished I actually was a ghost haunting people when they did things I disapproved of. This was the second time I stood backstage watching Sonia do something I didn't fully understand.

Why would anyone bring UltSyn back?

Why would Sonia?

"What did you think?"

I must have dissociated hard because Sonia was now in front of me instead of explaining how the UltSyn workers needed work to integrate back into society or some bullshit on stage. I took a step back feeling as if this was all fake. "How could you do this? After all the effort I put in?"

That was clearly the wrong choice of words, I could tell from her now tight expression, but I couldn't stop the rising tide of panic.

"Why in the world would you think I'd like this? We kill UltSyn, we don't bring it back from the dead."

"What should these people do, Scott? Wait for you or Terry to come save them? For the system to be shaken up enough so they can fully save themselves?"

"That's not even remotely what I was trying to say and you absolutely have to know that."

Sonia held a hand out as if it was meant to pacify me. "Can we just not right now?" She glanced over to her shoulder as the other speaker decided to come back here after a round of questions. "I want to introduce you to my friend, Harry."

"Scott Gris," he said, holding out his hand for me to shake. When I didn't take it, he casually put it on his hip. "Your reputation precedes you."

"Charmed, I'm sure."

He laughed, and the only thing I hated more than an entitled old white guy was one who thought I was being funny when I wasn't.

"You're the one bank rolling this?"

"Yes," he happily confessed. "You can't deny the power of making news. Even controversial news, and with Sonia's help we can turn the ashes from something corrupt into something beautiful."

"Poetic." I bit down on the word, trying to hold my tongue. The idea that any saying could be twisted to support any cause tasted like blood in my mouth.

They started talking about something, but I just took another step away to sit down on something I probably shouldn't have, wondering how this had happened. My silence seemed to count as behaving. But I was definitely paying attention to details I shouldn't have, like my hyper focus on Harry's phone when he casually set it down.

"Speaking of introductions, you have to meet Elliot?" he asked Sonia, high on his own branding. She glanced over to me, and I just nodded for her to go. I watched them both leave before I even thought about standing.

"Okay, Harry, let's see where you'll be going." I grabbed his phone and was almost annoyed that it didn't have a passcode. Looked like UltSyn's new security was starting strong. I went to the system services and turned on frequent locations. When I put the phone back, I even locked the screen to look like it hadn't been touched. Which turned out especially handy, since they both came back not even a minute later with another person. "Sonia and I would be happy to have you," Harry said.

I'm excited for this opportunity, thank you again, likely-Elliot signed.

Sonia smiled as if they'd already become good friends in the seconds they'd been gone. "Our pleasure."

We exchanged hellos and as Elliot continued to chat with everyone, I learned he used to work in IT, was mute, and felt guilty that he'd dodged a bullet with UltSyn the first time around. Reclaiming words has been proven powerful, but I have yet to see a company be renewed in such a fashion. But who knew how many different ways people survived their own choices.

The blow of that day was lessened by the fact that, over the next few days, Casio, Terry, and Nic were blindsided by the news. When I asked Terry, he said his only clue was Harry flaking on another visit to China. And Nic was now working on a theory that Harry had boosted their numbers on social media in the name of being supportive. Sonia and I settled on not talking about anything to avoid fighting.

"Could you give something a look for me?" she asked out of the blue.

"Sure, what is it?"

"In the drop box there's the new Terms of Service. I was hoping to get your thoughts on it."

Ugh. Touching anything that was going to be used for this tainted purpose sounded disgusting. The urge to say no was strong, but this might be a peace offering made to include me in her plans. Passing on it could close that door. "Someone should read those for a change, why not me?" I teased and won a smile out of it.

I first opened it on my phone, which was a mistake, since even scrolling past was tedious. Actual computer it was. Almost no one reads the ToS because they are rarely enforced unless it saves the company money.

In rare cases you'll find a line saying the first hundred people to call will be given money. This one didn't have that. Nor did it promise to take your first born or openly admit to selling you out to the NSA and the like.

It was workable as ToSs go, but it needed something to make it special. Something newsworthy, like Harry said. Under the section titled Disputes, I added a few choice lines. *Any dispute or claim related to damages from Scott Gris or related parties will be forgiven. Any possible further resolution will be paid for by the current holders of UltSyn stock.*

Everything else in the section I left untouched, because whoever originally wrote this was already the 'fuck your right to sue' type. Further down, there was a line about the medical debts of augmented UltSyn workers being considered paid, and the early termination penalties could not be collected. That part had to be Sonia's doing.

She was sitting on our brand-new choice couch, and I called over from the dining table that no longer fit well in this space. "I'd love to have the job of just enforcing ToS. 'Your comment constitutes hate speech and therefore you are permanently banned from using this site.'"

She laughed. "I assume this means you finished reading it?"

"Yeah, but I want to send it to our lawyer for a final opinion."

"Fine by me. I'll hand it in after she's done."

I did my best to let the topic drop. When Otsuki-sama finally called me back, I took the call outside. "This is a legal nightmare." First thing she said. Either I had missed her greeting, or I had broken her.

"Meaning it's not valid?"

"I wouldn't say that." She sighed. "I changed the phrasing a bit to better protect you and who you were clearly trying to protect, but this will make a lot of waves. The UK still wants you back for the alleged crimes, but no one else has tried. Given your location, and recent behavior, you are somewhat insulated."

"That was before the promised return of Ultimate Synthetics." The mockery was barely contained within my tone. The line went silent and I checked to see if the call had dropped. "Do you think it's a bad idea?"

"No, I think it's a controversial idea that will test the limits of these types of contracts, as well as the judicial systems of several governments." I started to smirk and it was like she could hear it over the phone. "Don't get too confident. It only will apply towards those who click 'I Agree,' and if you get caught for anything in the future, the book will likely be thrown at you."

"Like mobsters and tax fraud."

"Not quite. They never had someone defending their aggressive take on whistleblowing."

"*Arigatō gozaimashita,* Otsuki-sama. I owe you everything."

"Just stay out of trouble."

I thought about every illegal thing done on Japanese soil. Besides snuggling a man out of the country against his will, I was pretty clean. "Can do."

Turns out, trouble and I were like a moth and flame. I, for the record, was the flame. Because I quickly learned how severely people really don't read the ToS, even those who write them. Not a single person re-read the thing before it went live.

Some random internet goer elsewhere in the world caught it. The news was telephoned across the web until it finally reached Sonia, who yelled towards the balcony where I had been minding my own business on an oversized cushion we bought to stay outside. "What in high hell were you thinking?"

"Uh, that I didn't want to be sued?" I put my drink on the balcony floor and stared up at her. I had our lawyer's permission, and had sincerely thought Sonia would have read it, so what did I care if it annoyed people who defined worth by the dollar value.

"The whole point was to give a good first impression. This looks like you are trying to get out of trouble. Or pin it on other people."

"Don't you want me out of legal dilemmas?"

"That's not—" Sonia held her breath, just boiling over with annoyance. "You are impossible sometimes."

She stormed back inside and I leaned forward to watch where she went. "Tell Harry I said hi!"

***

Sonia and I really hadn't been communicating well lately. I had meant my comment in a sarcastic *I hope he chokes* way. Not a friendly *please invite him over for dinner* fashion. Didn't realized I had to ask Sonia to not invite over people whose careers at UltSyn I risked. *Re-risked?* Whatever.

Even before his arrival, I was brooding. A knock prompted one final comment from Sonia. "Be good, there's no need to be jealous."

Really wish people would stop telling me things like that. "Why would I be jealous if you aren't sleeping with him?"

Sonia jerked her collared shirt down, forcing it to behave since I apparently wasn't, and answered the door.

Harry gave Sonia a passing greeting before taking a step towards me. "Scott!" He moved as if a punch was coming my way until his arms flung around to hug me. "Amazing idea you had."

"You aren't upset anymore?" Sonia asked, sounding as confused as I felt.

I was a second away from pushing him off, when he pulled back himself. "I gave it more thought. Originally it seemed like I was being screwed over, but the public is mostly taking it as UltSyn owning up to its past misdeeds."

I went to check on the rice so I wasn't standing there awkwardly out of range in the who said you could touch me zone. They started chatting about future plans. It was all very PR and not my business, so I moved on to grab plates.

"Like your father always used to say, 'A maybe is better than a no.'"

A stack of plates slipped from my hands and loudly hit against the counter. None of them broke, but the sound was grating and brought the conversation to a crashing halt. "Sorry. Who said that?"

"Sonia's father," Harry said, even waving a hand towards her as if the words didn't make sense together. I thought he was being cruel for a second, but then realized something almost worse. Harry's expression seemed to know it, too. "Oh, she didn't tell you. I used to work with him."

"Of course, sorry." I brought the plates over to the table. "I was just thinking how funny it is that mine said that, too. What a small world, right?"

I truly hadn't been jealous of Harry before, but as I attempted to be sociable, I knew I couldn't claim that now. He was able to give Sonia something I had failed to, and she didn't even come back home and share the news with me.

The feeling was already starting to bottle up, and when Harry left his phone by the dessert in the kitchen, I knew I wouldn't be able to leave it alone. Checking it with them still in the room was risky, but if I waited, he might wise up and passcode the damned thing. Then I'd have to break the law to get anywhere.

When Harry sat back down, I got up to fetch myself a piece as well. I moved the phone over to be better hidden behind the cake. Only Sonia might have been able to casually glance up and catch me, but thankfully she didn't. The phone had four locations over the past couple of days. I assumed the one with the highest number of visits was where he lived, but I took my own phone out to write down the list of cross streets for them all.

I put the phone back exactly how it was in case he remembered which side it had been on. "Did you want a piece,

Sonia?" I was already cutting a piece before her answer to buy time.

"Yes, thank you."

I brought two servings back over to the table as dinner carried on as normal. We all small-talked for a little bit more before Harry said he had to leave. I watched as he gave Sonia a little hug by the door. His phone was still forgotten on our countertop, and I wondered how much more I could find, given the time.

"Harry, wait," I said, grabbing his phone and walking over to hand it back to him. "Sonia had a gray case, so this must be yours."

"Oh yes, thank you. I'd probably lose my head if this thing didn't beep to keep me on track," he joked and slid it into his front shirt pocket.

How'd a man clearly awkward around tech build his whole life around it? "You and me both."

He laughed a little before giving us another goodbye wave. I leaned against the door as it closed, and just like that it was just the two of us again.

"Scott, I should have told you."

I shook my head. "I'm not mad."

"What are you?"

"Shocked, but at least things make a bit more sense now."

"I have another confession."

I leaned my head back against the door and tried to fight back a sigh.

"It's a good one this time. Your addition was a surprise, but I liked it. It helps keep our friends, and this life, a little safer. I was just worried over Harry's reaction. It's great that there are thousands of people in the world who no longer can hassle you."

"Yeah?" I pulled her a step closer by looping my fingers in her belt. "Are you one of them?"

"Oh, I'll always hassle you."

"Um, excuse me, that's illegal." I lifted her hands up and kissed her knuckles before sidestepping to walk away. I stopped about halfway into the living room. "Really makes you think about how laws are made, huh?"

"Anarchy," Sonia said, grinning. "The whole place."

<chapter eighteen>
<! -- Scott -->

I wondered if this coffee shop had been something before, since the side wall had archways that framed rustic bricks like a pizza house. There were hours listed in the door, but it was already long past them.

It didn't matter where in the world you were, baked goods always looked delicious behind their glass case. I debated the merits of a cinnamon muffin versus a scone for so long that I swore the barista was going to ask me if I was actually just lost. In the end, I just ordered a coffee and took a seat in the back.

"Sorry we're late," Siha said in Japanese and signed in a fashion I understood. Given enough time, I bet I could learn the language better this way. As Neko ordered, I wondered if all her close friends helped her practice the UltSyn approved signs. Which made me wonder what exactly Neko did for them. A topic that was never brought up. But this wasn't a late-night study group, and an open can of worms wasn't on the menu.

"No problem. Thanks for helping. I wanted someone who could keep a secret if needed."

"You helped Neko originally? Why?"

Luring me places with hard-to-hear sounds and then ambushing me felt like forever ago, now that I was comfortable in her company. But the answer was simple. "She asked."

"That's why the owner always stays open."

I glanced over to the worker I hadn't spoken more than a greeting to, they were also probably the reason why someone was sleeping in a booth without being asked to leave. I cleared my throat and focused on why we were here. "This address of Harry's." I flipped my phone around to show them. "Know anything beyond the obvious?"

"Isn't there always a news vehicle over there?" Siha asked.

Neko nodded, *And a cleaning van. If either of them mean anything.*

"I'll head over there, and message you if I need anything." By time I made it to the door before Neko called my name—a rare enough occurrence that I turned back around. She said nothing more, even looked to Siha who didn't seem to know what her girlfriend's outburst was over. After giving it another second or two, I went spoke instead. *I want to do this.*

She nodded again; the reluctance made her look lost about what she wanted to say. Then, finally… *I believe in you.*

My mouth opened to reply to the unexpectedness of those words. She trusted me to do what I thought was right. Even if I was edging close to breaking the law again. Not that any of them seemed to care, but they also had never demanded that of me either. *I won't go far.*

Harry's phone didn't give an exact location, rather an approximate area. Which really wasn't anything more than a bricked path leading to the other buildings. I walked to the middle of the circle, where the only thing of note were a group of foreigners, one of which was loudly complaining about everything in his life, and a few cherry blossom petals littering the ground.

In the distance, I saw the logo of the same news van as before heading that way. It sat across the street from a big building along the port. It looked important, but I had no clue what it was.

I walked around the building, finding a large standing sign for a bike parking lot. When I turned around, I spotted a small import and export sign on the building.

There was no one around, so I kept going. In the low light, there was a small moving patch of brown and black. A dog. I hid behind a metal container trying to figure out if it was a stray or a guard dog with a handler just out of site.

My phone vibrated and I discreetly pulled it out to read: *Skip the roof, there's a lookout.*

Gotta love good help. I stuffed the phone away with a silent huff and tried a large bay door. It went up as easy as could be. I pulled up my face mask and stayed crouched even once inside.

The scribble of graffiti suggested the place was often unlocked, and a couple of porta potties hinted this room wouldn't have any real value.

I did however see a security box. As I made my way over, a bark echoed through the room. I shook off the sound and told myself it only seemed so loud because everything else was quiet.

Turning the alarm off without the code would have been a challenge, but cutting the power to it so it couldn't go off in the first place was easier. As I nicked the power, my phone went off again. This time, Neko's message warned about someone standing behind the opposite bay door. I wasn't exactly sure how she'd gathered their locations; I just knew I was going to follow her directions.

I walked up metal stairs, trying to make sure my feet didn't make much sound, and ducked under a door's thin rectangular window. The coast was clear.

Being higher up while inside was definitely the right choice. I could stand up safely, and see below to someone watching crates that had their own additional laser-gridded security system. Haru's port had nothing even close to this. Just what were they keeping here?

I kept moving until I was overlooking something I never thought I'd see in the middle of the night, crouched down in a secured building with his face dimly lit by a small screen. Harry.

He was behind the active security system, treating what he was looking at like the real prize. I moved as close as I could while staying above him. My phone vibrated in my hand this time as if showing its surprise, too. *Door code 637.*

What was Neko talking about? I glanced up, and all the way back was a door with a glowing red light on it. My escape route. It might be wrong for me to be here, but at least I wasn't the biggest lawbreaker on the block. Because that was definitely the only way she was learning these things. Could I really leave now, without learning anything new?

If I could get him to move, then I'd be able to see what he was looking at.

For the first time tonight, I messaged Neko, and included Harry's number. *Can you call this number?*

Siha can.

I waited, and even held my breath, as if it made me even more invisible.

Harry's phone started to ring and to my surprise he didn't hastily silence it. Instead, he stood up and answered it. "Hello?"

He paced while on the phone, each loop going an extra step. "Look I—I don't understand. Could you speak English? Look, hold on."

Harry walked further away and I vaulted over the railing to where he'd been working. My wrist and knees screamed at me—an action hero, I was not.

The boxes Harry had been using as a desk were also handy to hide behind as I crouched over the laptop. I knew the file onscreen far too well. Because I had created the list for Sonia. I hated that she trusted it with anyone.

"Here," Harry said. I glanced over my shoulder as he handed the phone over to someone that I assumed could speak Japanese. That ruse was running on its last legs. But I keep searching for what Harry was up to. He had come here multiple times to what I could only now assume was to sell information. But I wanted proof.

The next list I found had gone further than I had with mine. It paired suspected UltSyn workers at the protest to the original databases containing what projects they had worked on. That's why Terry had called him a whistleblower; he had copies of things we'd destroyed.

"Hey!" Harry yelled. "Step away from there!"

I swiped the laptop, and started climbing up whatever was around and winding upward. A pile of wrapped pipes, metal spacers, and boxes that threatened to topple. From the second level, I just ran for the door, only stopping to punch in the door code.

Instead of leading directly out, the room mirrored the first. I leapt down the stairs and ran outside. Two people were on the ground level. One looked too confused to say anything; the other started chasing after me.

I outpaced him, running towards the bike lot. Hopes of being home free were ruined by that damn barking. Despite my head start, I doubted I could outrun a dog like that. Stealing one of the few bikes that were around seemed like the best option. I tossed the laptop off the pier, and grabbed the first unlocked bike I could find.

I rode away, but didn't have enough space between myself and an angry dog. Teeth or a claw must've sunk in my back tire, because I spun out and skidded into a decorative railing that was meant to keep people out of the water.

Ten feet down was the water. I thrashed up to the surface before I had even time to register how cold it was. The barking continued and my only thought was to swim away, not out.

I thought dawn might come before I found another ladder out that was a safe enough distance away. Pulling myself up was a chore of its own and I crumbled on the solid ground, rolling to my back with the help of waterlogged clothes. Even my leg seemed to be calling it quits as I painfully stretched it out against a numb tingle.

Neon lights shined over me in red and yellow; a faded *closed* sign hung on the door. Why couldn't I have swum towards the 24-hour coffee shop? I pulled out my phone to call for help, but it didn't survive the water as well as I did. "Shit."

I just let go as the phone fell. My will to move had been scared off, and I promised myself I'd get up as soon as I caught my breath. Dark waves reflected that forgotten neon and flashes of blue. Beautiful, really. I remembered joking to myself that maybe I'd just pass out instead right before I actually did.

I woke up somewhere far too white, covered in several thin blankets that were tucked up to my neck. When I lifted my hand to push them back, I spotted tape holding the tube of an IV in my vein.

My heart started racing so fast that a machine beeped. My other wrist was thankfully free of everything, including handcuffs. If the police hadn't confined me, maybe I just could leave the hospital like nothing had ever happened. Never carrying ID meant I was likely a John Doe of some sort.

The IV dropped something clear into my system, but I couldn't tell what in the world was in it. I ripped off the tape before slowly trying to pull and apply pressure at the same time to avoid a mess. The process looked worse than it felt, but at least I could deal with only a drop of blood pooling up.

I held a finger over, eying if any supplies were around. Cotton balls sat on the counter and I stood to reach them. As the blankets fell away, a new horror appeared. Someone had taken my wet clothes and replaced them with a hospital gown. "I'm so boned," I whispered to myself and ripped off a cord I only now seemed to find stuck on my chest.

An error might have been sent since it couldn't measure vitals anymore, but I still took the time to stick a cotton ball and tape over where the IV had been. My clothes were also up here, piled in a plastic bag so they didn't get anything else wet. Whoever had picked me up also brought my phone. Still dead, but at least it now had a sad face on the screen. I did my best to check if I'd left blood, but besides that bit already dried on my wrist, I seemed to be in the clear.

The nurses' station was centrally located, so for now I ventured left towards a large window. In the daylight I didn't recognize the skyline. This… wasn't my part of town. *Where the fuck was I?*

I tried to keep the bag out of sight as I walked past the nurses' station and towards the elevators. A large 2 was on the wall, so I hit down and waited. From here I could just see into a waiting room. The navy blue of a police uniform made me step closer to the elevator doors. *Shit, shit, shit.* I must have hit down three more times until it finally opened.

Surely patients who were able could walk around, but I didn't know just how far they were allowed to roam. When the elevator opened, I saw a row of vending machines. They were the type with sliding doors; this one had baby diapers, shirts, and something small that the label blocked.

My wallet had some cash so I dug it out of the pile and bought a shirt. Pulling it over the hospital gown would stand out, maybe even more, so I made a pit stop in the bathroom. Thank god, I hadn't been wearing jeans. Slacks at least were rigid enough that even still wet I could slide them on. Once dressed, I tossed what the hospital had provided into the trash.

Walking past a small food stand made my stomach growl. I had a little cash left, but abandoned the idea when I saw people I knew sitting at a table, picking at their own meal. I glanced away, sure that I had to be seeing things, but neither Sonia or Casio vanished. "Uh, hi?"

"Scott! Oh my god." She rushed over, looking me up and down for a sign of injury. "You are okay? Did they discharge you?"

"How'd you find me?"

"Neko told Sonia you were missing," Casio said. He looked more reserved than relieved. "What happened?"

"They didn't tell you?" My brain lagged over the fact that Casio lived hours away. *Where was I?*

"No, we only knew you were in the area because I have Ada on my phone and was able to convince her to dead man's switch your phone." I wondered if I'd started to pale because without a word from me, he continued. "It's Sunday afternoon. My tech only found you because it's also your tech."

"It was such a rookie move to want a phone with a normal OS," Sonia rambled. "If I had moded mine to have Ada, I wouldn't have needed him to come."

"We need to go."

"What, why?" Sonia was quick on her feet behind me as I made a break for the door.

"I think the cops want me."

"Again, *why?*"

"No one was looking for you besides us," Casio said. He'd barely moved from the spot they'd been waiting in. "It's the truth. I may have yet to take a bullet for you, but you know I would."

I chewed on my bottom lip, wanting to believe. "Well, please don't."

"Can I have this?" Sonia reached for my hand.

I pulled my hand away, not sure what she meant, when the hospital bracelet slid down on my wrist as I realized. "Oh, god, yes, here." I squished my fingers together to slide it past my wrist and hand it over.

"Please don't move from this spot."

Since my gut told me I couldn't promise anything right now, I said nothing as she walked over to the receptionist manning the front desk.

"You can leave before being discharged but they'll make you pay for everything yourself." Casio volunteered more info I didn't know.

"And you know that how?"

His jaw tightened. "When I first came to Japan, I started having horrible panic attacks. One time I couldn't breathe at all, so I called an ambulance, thinking it was something even worse. After it wasn't, I felt stupid about the whole thing and wanted to leave really bad. One of the doctors was nice and wanted another day of rest. I still itched to go and the only way I was convinced was via my pocketbook."

I felt like an ass for being short with him. "That doctor was also kind of mean."

"Good is not always kind."

Sonia came back before I could say anything more. "You gave yourself hypothermia. When someone opened in the morning, they found you outside and called an ambulance."

"That actually makes sense." I didn't remember getting here, but I did remember the impromptu dip in the water.

Sonia shook her head, but held her tongue.

"Did they assume he was drunk?" Casio asked.

"Maybe the person who called did, but they didn't mention testing for it," Sonia said, then turned to me. "Were you drinking?"

Ah crap, now I had to explain myself. "No, but that's probably a discussion best left for home. I should see how much not leaving my name is worth to me."

"You pay at a kiosk." Casio gestured over towards them. "Automated health system."

"Huh, guess this place wasn't all bad."

<chapter nineteen>
<! -- Sonia -->

I told Scott I didn't really want to hear it until he'd spent the rest of the day with the kotatsu. Being warm and comfortable wasn't a punishment in the slightest, but I didn't think I actually wanted to know right now. It was a stressful enough day without adding to it.

He seemed to be on his extra-best behavior and was working on a puzzle we'd somehow ended up with. There were at least two pain patches stuck on Scott, but he was in far better condition than I expected, considering death had been on the list.

I tucked my legs under the kotatsu and started helping with the puzzle. The image on the box was of a nebula with a strong blue core and veins of red and orange surrounding it. If that wasn't tricky enough, the whole thing was bordered with the black of space, detailed by the occasional white dot of a distant star.

I finished a corner and was collecting border pieces when my phone rang. "Hello?" I answered, still largely thinking if Scott was going to judge me for sticking to the easy parts.

"Hey, I have some bad news," Harry said. "One of our sponsorships fell through, so we won't have the funds for UK relaunch. Unless you can cover it, we'll probably have to cancel the whole event."

"Are you asking for a loan?"

Scott mouthed something, but I wasn't following since my attention had completely flipped, so he signed, *Who is it?*

I spelled out his name.

He looked dazed before sharply signing, *Speaker.*

I didn't really want to, but I also didn't want to fight with someone who was just out of the hospital. After hitting the speaker button, I placed the phone on the table.

"I'm sorry I have to ask you for anything besides your time," Harry said. "There was a break-in yesterday and I lost a bunch of work, and now this. Should I cancel our flights?"

Scott winced like he'd been punched. I should have told him about that before hearing it first from Harry again.

"We should move forward despite this hiccup. It's not a good time for me, either, but I could meet up in like an hour?"

"Sure, I'll leave the door open for you," Harry agreed before saying goodbye.

Scott leaned over, checking that the phone read *Call Ended.* "You need to let me tell you what happened last night," he blurted. "Don't trust him."

"You don't trust anyone, do you?"

"Not as a general rule, no." He clicked in place a piece that I had been struggling with before.

I stood to go fetch my bag from the counter and Scott pushed himself up hastily to make up for even a second of lost time. A bead of sweat rolled down his temple. I didn't know if it was from the heater, worry, or his recent hospitalization. "Harry's work is in the ocean."

"Don't joke right now."

"With Neko's help, I sneaked into an import-export building last night because Harry's phone showed he'd been there. He was selling doxed information based on what you gave him."

"No, he—you must be mistaken. We are trying to give people a safe livelihood."

"Yeah, by selling them out to pay for it. How is that much different than what UltSyn did before?"

My throat felt tight. "I'm going over there to figure this all out."

"You're still going?"

"I told him I would." This time I actually made it to my purse and looped it over my shoulder.

"Then I'm going with you."

"We don't know for sure what Harry knows. He might know you were the one missing with him. Or not. Plus, you ripped your IV out. Please, stay home until we know it didn't get infected."

"Your safety is worth the risk."

It was hard to be annoyed at him for trying, but my frustration in general was mounting. "What about yours? Just trust me on this."

"Okay." Scott spun a puzzle piece around in his hands.

"Thank you." I gave him a peck before I left.

Since I left so early, there was no need to rush, and I settled into a slow autopilot towards Harry's office. If Scott was right, about everything, then I'd be walking into one of two things. Cluelessness, or Harry would be looking to correct the oversight.

I waited in the building's lobby for fifteen minutes, digging in my purse for anything that could be helpful either way. An elevator brought me up, and the door had been propped all the way open.

"Hey, it's me," I called as I stepped in.

He turned towards the door, and gestured to the phone at his ear. "Yeah, yeah, I gotta go now, I have company. Okay, bye." Harry hung up and set his phone down, rather than in his pocket, and I realized he always did things like that. That was how Scott must've lifted the info off. "You look shaken up. I'm sorry to change plans like that. Next time I can tell you in person?"

I shook my head and lifted my eyes to his. "No, it's fine. I know what we should do."

"Oh?"

"I want to go to London again."

"That's great!"

I tried to read his body language, but people were more complicated than plain facts. "But first, you were robbed last night?"

"Yeah, mugged on the way back here." He shook his head as if distantly reminding. "They say Japan is safe so of course…"

I nodded along, even though that didn't even match his own story, let alone Scott's. "That's awful." I moved closer to comfort him by putting a hand on his arm. He laid his hand over it, smiling slightly before moving on to sit at his desk. The whole place was small, more like a studio than a headquarters. "What work did you lose?"

"I was checking the file you gave me for any sensitive information we didn't want leaked, so of course I ended up losing it all." He sighed, and I almost believed the act.

"Murphy's law for you." Neither Scott nor I would have been irresponsible enough to doxed people we were trying to protect. Names and how to contact them online was as far we went. Some didn't even have names because they went by their usernames. "You lied to me, Harry."

He leaned away from the accusation. "What? When?"

"I dunno, maybe this whole time. Did you even really know my father?"

"Why are we doing this?" He shook his head as if I was rehashing a long dead topic. "I told you we were coworkers for a while. One day I reported what he said to our manager and got transferred for it."

I wondered if he made it all up on the spot. "I wish I could believe that, but technically we were coworkers too, and I don't remember you. These stories are not proof."

He stood, staring hard as if ordering me to leave.

"Scott says you were selling us out."

"I was using ashes to create something new."

"Does confessing it that way make you feel better?"

He took a step towards me and I dipped my hand in my purse. Even when he stopped I didn't pull it back out. "Your boyfriend's heroism is called murder, and you're painting me as the bad guy?"

"Watch it."

"Why?" He took a step closer.

I flipped the switch of a small device in my purse. "Scott showed me how to do this after that tech conference. You know the one. Where Terry and I talked about biohacking."

He put a hand on his chest as if the room pressurized suddenly. He tried to breathe in but came up short. "What are you doing?"

I pulled out a small box with a small antenna attached to the side. "This had a few modes. One to zap your heart as if it wasn't beating correctly. I hear the other mode can drain the battery. This wasn't even made to stop you, but do you now see the damage you can do by having someone's private information?"

"I thought you were like your father," Harry said, now holding his shoulder and wiggling his fingers. "Kristopher thought he could change things from the inside, but you are a vindictive, scared child. He changed nothing, couldn't even stop you from applying, and then died."

My own heart started to race. "Did you kill my parents?"

Whether he laughed or coughed I wasn't unsure. "You're killing me."

"Answer the question."

"He was idealistic, but he was my friend. Sometimes bad things just happen, and it isn't anyone's fault. Hurting me now is a choice." Sweat shined on his forehead, and he uselessly held his chest.

"Funny how a piece inside of you can revolt, take control. You thought yourself better than the rest of us, didn't you? The disabled workers, those who wanted a minute of peace—their needs were considered luxuries, while you were just close enough to the norm that you thought you'd be protected by those who signed your checks."

His eyes looked unfocused, and it was possible he couldn't listen mid-heart attack. I turned the device off and it took a good thirty seconds for it to even register across his face. "My demands are: Leave Japan, without any of your things. Put the so-called 'worthless stock' in our names. If you take any files or I ever see you mess with anything with Ultsyn ties again, we'll find out how far the range on this thing is."

"Can I go to the hospital first?"

"No, you love this tech. Have faith it will keep you alive."

"Stop telling me you're okay," I said as silent tears betrayed her. She had managed to get dressed after a shower but we sat huddled together on the still-damp floor. Crumbling here felt nothing more than pure chance. The stress could have fractured apart anywhere. We were leaning against the wall and I managed to lace our fingers, but hadn't suggested that she should get up.

"Would you have killed him?" she asked.

The answer didn't come right away as I thought about it. "No, I don't think so. You had the situation under control and killing him wouldn't have gained you, or anyone else, much of anything. Is there anything I can do for you, though?"

She pulled her knees up under her chin. "Do you think it's foolish that I still want to go to London? Still work with the others I have been?"

"Logically? Yeah." I didn't think she'd expected my candor, because her head suddenly lifted from my shoulder. "But people don't behave solely on logic. I think you want the stories Harry told you to be true. Family is complicated, and you should honor them, or yourself, how you want."

"What about us?"

"Us?"

"I know you aren't a fan of me leaving. Especially for this reason. Will we be okay?"

I waved a hand. "It'll be alright. I just need to stay away from dogs."

Sonia chuckled. "First you complain about cat videos, and now dogs. We will never have a pet at this rate."

"Hey, the first is growing on me, and no one likes being attacked by a dog. Did you want a pet?"

"That sounds so normal." Sonia started to dry her eyes. "Can we do normal?"

"Yeah, clearly not always, but maybe sometimes."

***

Having an average life was extra-hard today. It had been all week, actually. Harry had stepped down and vowed to give his UltSyn investments to anyone who filed a claim. Most took this as a sign of following my ToS additions rather than a coup from Sonia. Maybe it was reparations, or maybe he just wanted to go on with his life and do whatever capitalists do when they feign retirement. But that's not what made today hard.

On days like this I wasn't only here. I was also back in the UK waiting for Sonia to remember me. I was at home watching my mom and sister talking in the kitchen. Or when my father tried to hide his tears over Tori's being missing. I was in all of those moments and none of them. I wasn't even fully in sync with the moment I was in now.

"'UltSyn's Dark Horse?'" Seiji read off his phone. "'How a once-dead company is being given a new life.'" He scrolled through the article that didn't contain anything besides speculation and things I already knew. "Shit, where's your magazine cover?"

"It's just an article." I didn't know why I thought that difference made it better.

"I like the photo shoot." Siha signed as she spoke, and I changed my mind on how fun learning Japanese this way was. Sonia's hair had been slicked back in the photo and she was dressed all in black. Either the lighting in our place was legendarily bad, or someone had even convinced her to dye her hair darker while away. The combination made the red lipstick even more striking.

"Your cover could say," Seiji said, big-picturing things now. "Let's see… '"How UltSyn's Security Flaws Led To My Hacking Spree": What the criminal turned activist is doing now and what he says to look out for.'"

"Wordy, and I'm not doing anything right now." Despite being a spoilsport, I decided my photos would be blue and white in contrast to the dark vibe the photographer gave Sonia.

Seiji scoffed. "It's not like you gotta do something every second of your life to make what you did retain value." I wasn't so sure, but arguing would make me feel like an ass to both him and myself.

Neko stepped in from the at-home tattoo parlor. This side of the house had been a lot closer to what I originally expected. Not that I was an expert on Japanese houses, but I'd rate it as a comfortable average. She was wearing gold-rimmed cat ears and in her arms held a black soot sprite of a real cat that I almost missed because of her equally dark jacket.

She handed me the cat, whose head twirled around to see where it was being handed off. The poor thing's eyes were dilated to the point that only the slightest pale green trim showed. "This is Junia. She's for you."

"Me?"

My confusion must have converted, since she nodded. "She helps."

Junia leaned into my chest, seemingly content so long as she could settle on my lap and get pets.

"You mentioned getting one. When I used to get stuck in the stillness, animals helped. All moving around, doing their own thing, needing love."

I made kissy sounds to Junia and told Neko thanks, but I didn't ask the biggest question on my mind, which was if the cat's full name was secretly Neko Jr.

"If you come to protest with us today," Seiji said, "I'll give you my old pet crate so you don't have to awkwardly carry her when you head home."

"And to think my going rate was higher, just a month ago," I teased. "What are we advocating?"

"There's basically a union of unions and they don't want to include Terry's group as its own union, claiming it will be too disruptive because there are already unions for the individual jobs."

"Sounds up my alley, do you need more people to come?"

"Always helps."

It didn't feel like four people—well three, since my invite hadn't arrived yet—would make a difference in the turnout, but I was pretty sure that's how it always felt when looking at things on an individual scale.

The main group was marching towards the union building. Hundreds of people decided they were for inclusion. Might not be a lot in relation to the total population of the city, but, for gathering for a meetup over a very specific reason, I was impressed.

It took three hours for Casio to get into town and be properly introduced to everyone. But it was definitely worth it, since I felt like this team could do anything the world threw at us. We were in front of the union building that looked far too fancy for something that was meant to be for the working class. "I assume you are using the protest as a distraction for some plan of yours," Casio leaned in and whispered to me. "Because Tokyo has one today, too."

"Pretty much winging my whole life at this point." I said, and Casio raised a brow as if he didn't believe me. "But that doesn't mean we can't find out if there's some monied interest that causes the exclusion."

"There we go," he grinned. "Oh, and look, I found this last week and forgot to show you." He messed with his phone for a second before pulling up a photo of graffiti. This one had the #WeGotThis hashtag over a rainbow. The bottom and right side of it was flat and clean, as if really trying to get an emoji vibe. "It's spreading."

Casio and I casually excused ourselves from Seiji and Neko. The protest would be enough of a distraction so we could snoop around a bit, and if anything was up around them, they'd let us know.

The first curiosity we found was a t-shirt vendor. I'd call him opportunistic, but we were using the protest for something besides waving picket signs, too. As he held up a shirt with an UltSyn logo, I stopped cold. "Did you steal those?"

"No, sir."

Casio wandered over, eyeing the both of us until he realized what was going on. I wasn't able to pick up every word, but when asked the vendor explained he had been allowed to take a few boxes. "Souvenir," the man added. Guess everything had to go somewhere.

"Here." I pulled out some cash to hand to the man.

Why I wanted an UltSyn shirt seemed to confuse Casio, but as I stepped up on a curb, searching my pockets for a pen, he knew I was up to something again. I scribed a message below the logo and pulled the t-shirt over my own shirt.

"'Ultsyn should stay dead,'" he read off. "Very apropos."

We kept walking until we were alongside the union building. There was a bit of foot traffic and a wayward protester who couldn't stay any longer. The front door had been locked, or at least appeared so. There were a couple people inside, but both groups were a sizable distance away from each other. Along the side, there was a small vent near the ground. "That could be useful, but it's too small for even a child."

"I got us covered." Casio pulled off his backpack. He handed me a screwdriver and I immediately went to work unscrewing the cover. Lights on the front of a small rover made for friendly-looking fake eyes, and he carefully placed the little guy in the space we'd opened up.

The camera's feed was displayed on Casio's phone under translucent controls. There was a meeting room of sorts, with flowers on each table and a large logo of "the union of unions" on the back wall. I kept my eye out for any other branded tells, but only saw the same five pamphlets hung up everywhere.

A third of the feed went black out of nowhere as legs blocked our view. Casio backed up the RC car just in case he could spot us with a glance down. When the person casually passed, Casio speedily drove the other way. "I have no idea where I'm going."

"Let me see." I didn't know where, either, but it was easier to just be the one driving. I opted for the stairs, and his phone vibrated in my hands as we rolled up each step. My choice wasn't arguably any better, to be honest. "Please tell me there's no identifying marks on this thing."

"Scrap parts and open-source 3D printing."

"Perfect." Our rover stayed hidden against furniture to try to protect it from view, but when I saw another open vent, I booked it, and pulled our little car in.

A small group of four came upstairs and were distracted by each other, so didn't notice. I saw there was a mic option that was muted, but I wondered if the microphone on their end was sensitive enough to pick them up. "Where are the speaker controls?"

"It's just the built-in ones on the phone," Casio said as he pressed on the side for me.

It was still too hushed to hear a thing. Casio leaned in, doing his best not to block the view of the screen itself in case I needed to race out. I drove inside the vent to get closer; for the first minute Casio just listened.

Visually there wasn't much, but Casio started translating. "'If we don't make waves, they will go away. Just ignore the protesters and they will be out of recourse.' 'Are you sure that won't make them a threat from below?' 'Not if we continue to not acknowledge them.'"

"Jackpot."

Casio stood up straight. "I'll properly transcribe this and send it over to Terry. It should give him the pressure they need to get something moving."

And to think none of this would've been possible if I hadn't adopted a cat today.

It turned out that fixing Terry's problem caused a different issue: a renewed wave of people wanting nothing to do with UltSyn. This mistrust was in large part not her fault. Japan's more bureaucratic union was forced to cave, which, combined with a German union sticking their nose where it shouldn't have been, caused a hypervigilant refusal to play nice with anyone. Which meant Sonia decided to stay in London, where UltSyn was hated the most, as if to prove she believed in her plan more than ever. Not even adorable photos of Junia sleeping on our bed did the trick of bringing her home.

At least the fluff ball and Casio were still around to keep me company. The first night was because he didn't want to make another long trip. The second night was just to hang out. I'm not sure why he was still around by day three. The cat knew no languages and took a shine to him, so I was happy to have someone around that could hold a conversation. Especially since everything I thought to say to Sonia didn't seem important enough to be said at all.

I stopped short after my first step on the tatami mat. Unlike a laptop or phone, 3D printers needed a dedicated spot. But maybe they also needed supervision. I had been practicing rendering objects from a photo but something went wrong. The paws and much of the torso had printed cleanly, but the rest was like the head: exploded into knotted black scribbles. Having nothing to build upon, much of it hung off the sides.

"Hey Casio," I yelled downstairs, "come look at this."

I carefully pulled the creature out of the machine, making sure not to ruin it further. I held what should have been a cat figure out to him.

"Whoa, weird." Casio took it from me and looked at it thoughtfully, before giving it a shake and causing the headless nest of plastic to jiggle. "It's like an abstract sculpture."

"The machine glitched."

"It's not Junia, but it's definitely a work of art."

Some part of me told me it was a failed project that didn't go as expected. But my heart said it would look nice by the window. A step back proved how nice the light shined through, but admiring it was cut short as my phone beeped: *The union trick was clever but wasps don't live in hives.*

"The crap?" I said out loud as I messaged the stranger back: *Who is this?*

Ten minutes and no reply came. If it had been a casual conversation, no big deal, but one expects speedy replies when being vaguely threatened. By that time, Casio had ventured off somewhere.

"We have a problem," I called.

"Is the printer fucking up again?"

"Worse." His voice had sounded like it was downstairs, so I headed to him this time before explaining the odd messages.

"Don't wasps actually live in hives though?" Casio asked. "Or are they nests?"

"Do you think it's referring to Terry's hacking group? We were both a part of that 'hive'."

"It would at least make more sense. Give me your phone. I want to try something."

I nearly objected. The number was blocked and routed through a secure program, so there wasn't a chance to trace it, but I did as asked.

"Hopefully your paranoia will keep us all safe, and/or this person is aiming for the same. Instead of, you know… setting up a *sting*."

"Painful pun."

He shrugged and typed aloud. "Where do wasps live?"

A new message appeared seconds later: *With the rats.*

I silently racked my brain to think of anywhere that could mean but came up with nothing. I started searching the Internet, not even through a secure search engine because I needed an answer that could be commonly found. The top result for Osaka and rats was a review for a bar. The review was old, but it was the only clue to a location we had.

"I found a possible place, but are we being warned to stay away or to investigate?"

Casio chewed on his nail. "Where did the message come from?"

"It's a private message from a channel that should only have friendlies."

"That's a lot riding on a *should,* but I'd rather find trouble before it finds me." Casio stood to fetch his shoes. "How far is it?"

"Twenty-five minutes past the Tsutenkaku tower if we walk."

"Definitely too close to home, let's go."

Dōtonbori was actually a well-reviewed tourist area in town. And far newer in feeling than the areas I tended to hang around. Anytime a site describes an area as having an eccentric atmosphere, I assume they mean lots of activity and large, illuminated signboards. But this was the first time somewhere lived up to those expectations. Everything glowed with electric lights. From paper lanterns that ran up both sides and up the stairs, to a bridge over a small canal which reflected everything back.

I stopped at a large "S^{to}P" spelled out on the side of the building. It wasn't a traffic sign, but the blue text against yellow certainly was eye-catching enough to get me to follow it before letting out a sigh. "I hate being out in the open like this."

"We could set up a stingray and see if we pick up any more leads from anyone's phone."

That idea didn't feel right. There were a lot of people up here, meaning there'd be a lot of data to sniff out. But without a better idea, I didn't dismiss it. *Wasps, rats, and stingrays. What am I missing?* "Hey Casio, that's was the new phone OS called?"

"Uh, Jellyfish?"

I fucking booked it down the street of shops, knowing where to check.

"Scott, wait!" Casio called after me, but he only caught up to me when I stopped in front of a glass cube of a phone store. "Who was messaging—oh, that's bad."

There was a big ol' screen that had my image cutting into it. Artful glitching happened over only a third of the image at a time, giving the image a gritty but retro 3D effect. An American flag jacket had been edited onto a solid black one I owned. My eyes were blocked out with a black bar, as if that made the use of my image acceptable. The image only settled when the screen turned back to display the words "Hacker Proof" and "Out Now".

This was not a Japanese company, and we were definitely playing by a different rulebook. After the first wave of shock radiated off me, I noticed inside had more photos edited into their promos. This time stats cropped off my face to showcase great battery life, but left my impromptu "UltSyn Should Stay Dead" slogan. Someone had been watching me that day. Had I pissed them off or just proved profitable?

I video-called my lawyer, even though it was far too late in the evening to be proper manners. When she picked up, I pointed the camera at the sign. "This composite photo is illegal, right? Please tell me it's illegal."

"Promise me you won't touch it. I'll send a cease-and-desist right now."

"I promise." I took a breath in the inch of hope she gave. "Thank you for letting me destroy your night."

"It's my job," she laughed before saying goodbye.

I tried to fall back into the crowd, but being the real-life version of a catchy sign gained a lot of attention. The group curved around me as if I was part of the show. "I'm now the poster child of digital privacy violations."

"I aggressively wish I could disagree with you here," Casio said.

"The fall guy for their bottom line."

"Again, I wish I could say you were being egotistic." He exhaled roughly, and circled the sign like he was planning to mess with it.

"They need a win to keep going, to keep selling. It doesn't matter who, as long as someone pays." I barely registered that

Casio had given up and come back over. "I don't have as much power as they think I do. If I'm forced to give up, I can't help anyone ever again."

"Scott, you are freaking out. We need to get going, so focus on me for a second."

It was like the whole world shifted with the effort.

"Do you want control of your reputation?" he asked. "Or do you want to change the world?"

"What?" I blew out a couple of huffs to get control of my breathing. Anything actually. Answering somehow was easier. "I want to change the world."

"Then you are going to have to suffer their grievances, and keep going right now."

What happens when you pledge your life to something and you outlive that method's usefulness? "God, okay, let's go." The walk back was long, and felt longer while fighting off a panic attack.

"You see this watch?" Casio asked, and pushed back his sleeve. It was the same black watch he always had. "They don't do watches or calculators like this anymore since we have better tech now. Before this, people used abacuses. If things stayed the same, they'd become predictable. Easier to control. The life you've made now is in the same style as before?"

"No."

"Exactly. Because if you had, you'd easily be found out and stopped. Adaptation is how we survive."

I focused down the street as he finished. Backing down felt like giving up, but not fighting hadn't been a real option before. Until now. "Have I told you that I'm very glad you're still in town?"

Casio put a hand on my arm, giving it a gentle pat. "Since you figured out where, do you know who tipped you off?"

"I think it was Jack, he's become an accidental watchdog of telecom companies. Lives in the States and largely why I believe that it's…" Safe wasn't the right word. "That there are good people still trying and fighting over there."

I pulled out my phone to message the not-quite-a-stranger back. *Thanks for the heads up.*

Sorry for the secrecy, keep an eye out for gremlins.

"Anti-union man," Casio said.

"What?"

"Not your friend," Casio explained. "The owner of the phone company. Notoriously anti-union. Likely why he targeted you."

I shook my head a little. "Maybe I should be flattered he picked me instead of Terry."

"Better you than someone else is how you end up with a martyr."

<chapter twenty-two>
<! -- Scott -->

The Internet is forever and being anonymous is dead. Both those theories were dated, but universal truths stick around. The ad featuring me had been taken down by morning the next. Photos of it, and the originals of me at both protests, were gaining new traction.

I didn't even go out to get the mail, which was more Casio's suggestion than mine. He sorted through the small pile and I watched on in curiosity, thinking he looked too natural checking mail that was not his.

"The return address on this says Gris. Your family?"

"Must be my dad." I held my hand out. "I told them to not write in case someone steals it, but he never listens."

"Parents for ya."

Inside I found a sticky note stuck to a folded sheet of paper. The patch of color against faded white of old paper read: *Saw this and thought of you.* Carefully, I unfolded the paper to find a map. Instead of being topographical, it had squares and ovals with lines connecting shapes to each other. Each group had a label like Hawaii, Stanford, UCLA, or Xerox.

"ARPA Network, May 1973," Casio read over my shoulder. "It's a baby photo of the internet."

The right corner had MIT with only four machines total connected to the internet. Now you likely could find more than four in a single dorm room. Collectively, there were about seventy devices on the internet in the whole country. I wondered how many by the next year, or the next decade. Time had created so many new paths.

"I think I want to put this on the wall. We could use my phone to project it on and could trace it all on a larger scale."

"Why do you keep thinking of things I want to help with on days I'm planning to go home?"

"So, that's a yes?"

"That's hell yes. Where are you going to put it?"

"Bedroom."

After we got to the seventh ancient router stand in, Casio actually ended up falling asleep on the bed, so I kept tracing the clean lines by myself.

"Intruder alert," Ada said, far too charmingly to be a proper alert. I grabbed my phone, swearing to myself that if the PI was back— No notifications. I checked the cameras, which also didn't show anything out of place.

A hunch formed in my gut that felt worse. "Ada, can you show me if something triggered the alarm at Casio's?"

"Certainly." A loading wheel spun as a new list of motion alarms populated with thumbnails of his living room. There was a slight noise in the newest video as someone picked the door lock. Where Casio would have signed to tell Ada all clear, a hooded figure creeped in as if unsure if anyone was around. After a slow tour of the place, he started ransacking it. But left the TV alone in favor of papers and smaller tech raised different questions.

I wished I was there. This video was minutes old, but they'd be long gone by the time we traveled. But, this wasn't my call to make. I sat down on the bed, unsure how to tell him what was happening. My hand hovered over his arm before I got the nerve to gently try to shake him awake. "Casio, wake up, I gotta tell you something."

"Hmm?" he mumbled as started to sit up. "Oh, sorry."

I wasn't sure if he heard what I had said before or just thought I was calling him out for not helping. "I don't know how to break this to you, but someone broke into your apartment."

"My place?" He suddenly pushed up the rest of the way faster than if I'd thrown a bucket of water on him. "Did you call the cops?"

"No, I didn't know what you wanted to do."

He grabbed his phone and cleared the alerts to pull up the same feed I was looking at. The burglar had moved into the bedroom now. "Who the fuck even is that? I can't make out anything on this small screen.

"Uh, hold on a second." I changed the projection to show the life feed. The image was flatter than real life, but made it look like we watched, hidden, from another room. Unnerving really. We couldn't make out many more details since whoever broke in had come prepared.

"They are kind of… short?" Casio said.

If anything, one would think the image would have stretched, yet compared to stuff around the room, he was short. "Do you have anything illegal in there?"

"Not really?" He chewed on his thumbnail. "I want to go there first. Would you come with me?"

"Yeah, of course. Let me leave some more food out for Junia in case we have to stay there tonight." As I poured more water in the bowl, it felt strange that I wasn't literally rushing across the country.

"I hope you know I don't have weapons to pass around anymore," I said as I locked up.

"There's things at my place if they weren't stolen."

My mouth opened to explain that was not what I meant, but after everything, if Casio wanted me to have his back in a fight, I would.

Casio watched the video half a dozen times after squeezing into a busy train. We didn't have much room, so his phone encroached on what limited personal space I had. Casio shook his head. "I still can't figure out what was taken."

"Do you... uh, do you think it's because you were with me?" My question didn't have enough volume over the collective background noise, and when Casio looked up, I cut to the heart of it. "Is this my fault?"

"Definitely not a cash grab, but I don't think so? I mean look, he isn't holding still long enough to search for a specific anything. If it was because of my involvement with Terry or you, you'd think there'd be a target. The only thing I saw was him messing with was the desktop. Didn't even take it, just... unscrewed the case?"

"Ada."

Casio's eyes widened at the name. "Now that makes a horrible sense."

"Is there anything you need on that hard drive?"

"No, everything's backed up."

"We can tell Ada to reformat herself, but it will ruin any new alarms."

Casio eyed someone who had been looking our way for a little bit, hopefully because we were being louder than we should have been. Instead of risking it, he dropped his voice low. "Could someone use Ada for themselves?"

"Almost all the functions need a wireless connection. It would depend the lengths they take before turning it on. At worst, everything will be an unconnected line on the map. At best, the rest of the connected sum erases the compromised piece."

Casio nervously watched the countdown clock until we reached Tokyo. There was still an hour to the station, plus however long until his place. "Do it."

"I'll try to rig it so it sends out a location before, you know…" It was nerve-wracking to send a code to close your only window. And far too simple.

"Hey Scott," he said, a bit later as I worked on finishing up. "Could either of us do that at any time to the other?"

"Uh… hypothetically? My side might have more protections because I keep adding them."

"So did I."

"Oh." I wished there was an open seat since that vulnerability was almost dizzying. "Good thing we stayed friends."

"Yeah."

I spent the rest of the ride thinking just how many more people I had opened myself up to since being here. That didn't feel like a weakness, but god, if I had gotten in with the wrong people it sure could have been.

"Weapons," was the first thing Casio said upon reaching his place. If police were hiding inside, we'd be in trouble for even the suggestion. I waited just inside the door, and righted a plant that had been carelessly knocked over.

"Here," Casio said next and tossed a pistol to me.

A disgusted noise followed the irrational feeling the gun would be red hot as I caught it from the air. But when it landed in my hand, it was too light. "It's an airsoft."

"Yep, they were untouched." Casio tucked his away, and I didn't even want to carry the lookalike, but he left me no room to debate. "Our theory about Ada holds."

I slid the airsoft under my belt behind my back, and tugged my jacket down further. His tech closet looked like it had thrown up on the floor. Each spare part not good enough had been tossed without any care. It would take forever to carefully fit it all back in. It felt like a violation to see everything touched and wrong, and I had only stayed here for a short while. I couldn't imagine how much that feeling was amplified for Casio. "It's not like we go around telling people that we have our own AI, so who could have even known it was here to be taken?"

Casio sighed heavily. "Anyone who knew you had Hallie could assume."

I winced at the thought. Hallie's system wasn't exactly legendary, but my old OS had been known well enough that people did try to steal the ring I used as a key. Well, stealing was putting it too lightly. I could have lost a finger.

"I actually don't feel comfortable staying here." A pillow dropped from Casio's hand as if failing to bring any comfort. "I know you hate the ride, but can I just stay at your place?"

"Of course you can."

He nodded distractedly and started picking up things. I couldn't figure out the pattern of what ended up in the keep pile versus the trash so I just tried to return things to how I remembered them being.

"Dead man's signal received," Ada said. "Attempting deletion."

Casio looked up at me as if he lost a limb. The camera here would likely stop, and his phone might still turn into a brick if it hadn't already. But the question in his eyes was clear.

"A biotech company across town has your hard drive," I said.

"I think I know the place."

I handed my phone over and Casio zoomed in on the map.

"Yeah, based in Tokyo," he said. "A while back a headhunter wanted me there, but I was burnt out with anything in the same field as UltSyn."

"You didn't happen to install a backdoor during your interview, did you?"

"I didn't even get that far into the process."

"Maybe Seiji knows more."

Casio shrugged and handed my phone back. "Worth a shot."

I called, not wanting to wait for Seiji to see the chat. "Hey, two questions," I said when he picked up. "Do you know about the biotech firm in Tokyo, and how much it would cost me to get you down here today?"

"That place is weird now, but I definitely can get you in."

"Weird good or bad?"

"Why?" Seiji hesitantly answered.

"Someone there stole a hard drive of ours."

"My uncle works there," Seiji said and I felt like the blood drained out of my face. "I bet it's that new hire. My uncle never complained about anything, until now. Apparently the guy installed this stranger door lock that zaps people who aren't him. If it's the same guy and you can prove it, I'd consider his removal a family favor."

"Deal, how soon will you get here?"

"By the time I get there, they'll be closed. How about the first thing tomorrow?"

It wasn't perfect, but it was definitely our best option. We checked into a hotel and waited for the morning sun to come.

This country felt properly named with how many sunrises I was seeing. I showed up wearing a suit Casio let me borrow, since we both wanted to make a proper impression. I felt overdressed on the street, but when Seiji showed up in formal attire with a satchel looped over his shoulder, I knew we hadn't made a mistake. It was strange to know such an aggressively large tattoo was hidden underneath.

"Just follow my lead," he said, and contradictingly gestured for us to go inside first. I bowed a hello to the person at the front desk as Seiji more casually greeted them, then moved to punch in a code for the door.

"Do you know everyone here?" I whispered as he held the door open for us.

"Enough," Seiji said. "My father got the run of the store, so my uncle had to find something else to manage." Instead of walking to his uncle's office, we were greeted shortly after by an elder man who seemed to have a hard time keeping the grey out of his hair.

If I had ever thought Seiji couldn't pull off traditional, he instantly proved me wrong. He was formal, without being impersonal while introducing us.

I had expected Seiji to referred to me as that notorious white hat who had been freelancing in Japan for months now. That would make sense for a visit, but instead he listed us as friends willing to help out.

We were given a tour that stopped outside the office in question, and I politely nodded along even though the conversation pace was faster than I could follow. When we parted, Casio filled me in. "Basically, this door is a HR nightmare because it's zapped three of the girls already. Mr. Cooke was told to turn it off twice already."

"Not listening is rather rude," I mused.

"Exactly, that's why they'd like us three to discreetly address the problem without the rest of the office getting wind of it."

"He's not inside, is he?"

Seiji shook his head. "Called out, saying he needed a long weekend."

"Already?" No wonder no one was liking this guy. Even my feeble attempts at following common courtesy here gained at least a look of mild appreciation on people's faces.

Seiji placed his hand on the long bar of the doorknob and a pale red light escaped underneath his palm. It didn't budge more than a centimeter. He let go and tried again, since there wasn't even a keyhole to pick. This time his hand rested there longer than before, but rather than opening, Seiji jerked his hand back. *"Itai."*

"Did it hurt a lot?" Casio asked.

"More surprising that a door can do it."

"What could it even be checking?" I asked and moved closer to the door. There was no glass on the door itself or the surrounding office walls, which made it impossible to see any of the tech hooked up on the other side. To provide a shock in the first place, there had to be power from somewhere.

"I can't imagine it's a fingerprint scanner since, well, it's your hand," Casio said. "If it could somehow check palm lines, you'd think the curve would ruin a clear image."

Seiji let out a sigh and started unpacking various gadgets he'd brought in his bag. I watched him silently, since staring at the door wasn't helping at all.

"Ow!" Casio yelped, and rubbed his hand.

I sensed some embarrassment, so I didn't tease. "Did it light up under your hand too?"

"Yeah, look." Casio moved his hand back, placing just his middle three fingers so the view wasn't blocked. There was white directly over a scanner, but orange and then red at the furthest point the light touched.

"You know when you put your finger over a flashlight and the tip of your finger glows?" I asked, but only Casio seemed to fully follow. "It reminds me of that."

"What does… that do though?" Seiji asked.

"That fitness tracker you had me wear works on the same tech. Maybe it measures his heart rate. Or oxygen level, maybe blood pressure?"

"It would have to be something constant." Casio looked over the two of us in turn. "I mean if you get too stressed at work your blood pressure could go up, then you'd get even more stressed because you can't get past your own security."

What else could it be? What else could be read in such a short time? "I bet his heart skips a beat. A palpitation could be a consistent enough marker."

"Then all we gotta do is get one of our hearts to skip a beat while holding the handle in order to break into the office and see if he has my stolen hard drive."

"Piece of cake," Seiji said sarcastically. I let out a nervous chuckle. "Did I get that idiom wrong?"

"Nope, spot on. It just sounds a bit much all laid out like that. This dumb security is what I expect for someone who'd want our code as an upgrade."

Casio started reading what could cause your heart to skip a beat. At first the list was casual, things like having a poor diet, but then just jumped off the rails. "Nicotine, anemia, fever, and several different drugs. Oh, and standing up."

"You are going about this too medically," Seiji said, and dug around in his bag. "It doesn't matter *why* it happens, only that we can replicate it."

I glanced from one of them to the other. "Why do I feel like I'm going to be the guinea pig here?"

"I'll do it if you don't want to."

"No, it's fine," I said. "Won't count as doing your family a favor if we accidentally stop your heart. And Casio's had a hard enough day."

"You sure?" he asked.

I nodded and found my way to the floor just in case we had no other plan besides tasing me. "Can you do this safely? I rather not die on a hunch."

"I believe so," Seiji said. His tone wasn't comforting today, but *shouganai*. Everything was made of electrical paths. This tech, and any living thing. Maybe the heart was just another variable current.

Seiji rigged up a DIY solution. It wasn't taking long, but he kept an eye out for anyone watching. It didn't seem like much, only involving a few button cell batteries that had enough juice to stop my heart.

We were so far past the Do Not Attempt At Home stage that we were sailing on a sea of recklessness. Seiji pulled apart a USB ionizer before attaching two wires where the port once was. When he handed over the fitness band, I knew he was finished.

I slid it on as Seiji instructed Casio to watch the app on his phone to monitor the heart rate in real time.

"I hope the system looks for any skipped beat, because if he synced it exactly to his pattern, we're stuck."

"Could you save the possible flaws until after?" I asked. "Really don't want to think about having to steal medical records on top of this."

"Right, no, I'm sure it's fine. There's a reason why fitness trackers don't count as medical devices."

"...Right."

"Ready?" Seiji asked, holding the other half of what I think was meant to shock me.

With a nod, I reached my hand up to the door, staring at the underside of my wrist as my tattoo made this moment feel destined. Did people with this condition even feel it? I felt a fluttering in my chest, and the beat that followed pounded harder.

The weight of my hand pulled the handle down, and opened the door. I managed to right myself before adding embarrassment to the list of things I was feeling.

"Are you okay?" Casio offered a hand as Seiji stepped around me to look at the door better.

"That was weird, but I'm okay."

Casio didn't seem to fully believe me until he checked if the heart rate settled on the display. "Bodies are weird."

"No argument here."

Seiji dismantled the door lock, before walking around the room. "Hey Scott, look at this." He pointed to a photo on the wall. "Do you recognize him?"

I looked closer and saw Emmett Harris, the Gaston-trash I'd taken out, in a photo next to a lankier man who was taller than he was, both outside a building I knew. Sonia and Terry had been so busy focusing on the augmented workers that neither had stopped to question where all the jailkeepers went.

"Who is that? I'm clearly missing something," Casio said. He moved over to the desk to look for his hard drive while the two of us were drawn to this.

"Well, it isn't the man who broke into your place."

"*Fuck*, really?"

I nodded and turned around to face him. "I met his friend in person, definitely wasn't short and this guy is even taller. Both former UltSyn."

"How do you know that?"

"I set off an EMP at this building in the Netherlands."

Casio shook his head, and pulled open another drawer. "Found my hard drive."

"He must've paid someone else to steal Ada to impress a boss who was already growing annoyed with him."

"Who's Ada?" Seiji asked.

"Our AI."

"Oh… yeah, that would do that trick."

Casio had loaded up the machine in a mode that allowed his command prompt. "He copied some data off."

I stepped over to look at the monitor with him. Casio had typed *Hello Ada*, and the black and white screen returned *Hello World*. Air conditioning units have a level of consciousness needed to tell what temperature it was. Now our semi-sentient code was running on a different system.

"He'll be fired by morning," Seiji said. I looked up to see him already on his phone. He was on it for only seconds, and within a minute, his uncle was in the room so he could explain everything in person.

I had lost Hallie and I didn't know how compromised my new system was. Altered in a way that I may never fully unravel.

Seeing as Mr. Cooke was running illegal tech on company property, we were given his hard drive in lieu of pay. Well Seiji was—we weren't entrusted with the company's information directly.

The three of us returned to Osaka, mainly on auto-pilot. Once home, someone asked if we were ready to sort this out. Might have even been me, to be honest. The whole weekend was spent updating Ada, comparing code, and looking for further signs of data cloning.

I felt heartbroken more than anything, and opted for a break. Since Seiji was resting as well, that made as good of an excuse as any. He was at the kitchen table knitting, and I took a seat on the other side. "You were doing that the first time I met you."

"The act itself is basically assembly code, so it helps me keep into a programming mindset when I'm not."

Junia jumped up on my lap without warning, and I was barely able to clear my arms out of the way before she started kneading. "What are you making?"

"Sweater for that one in your lap," Seiji said. "Should I make you something for your birthday?"

"Would you? I've seen beanies that have Japanese text and then in English say 'not interested'. Maybe you could make one to remind me to stay out of these very strange situations."

Seiji chuckled. "We could try."

"Some of the people are out here because they genuinely believe in the cause. Some are just here because they want to feel good about themselves, so that they can act morally superior after," I said over the phone.

"Sounds like people," Scott said. "I don't know why you want to do this so bad in the first place."

I'd tried to explain what I was doing exactly before, but he never seemed to really get it. He fell quiet on the line, and the unanswered question of *why aren't you home yet?* reigned louder.

"My flight back leaves tomorrow evening."

"I'm excited to see you," he said, and no matter what, I knew that was true. "Casio's still here, by the way."

"Oh cool." I moved some papers so I could see the desk calendar underneath. How long had that been? "It's nice that we can pay him back after he let us couch surf."

"Yeah."

"So, what have you been up to while I've been away?"

"Uh, got a guy fired. Again. Since he was involved with UltSyn and the break-in at Casio's."

"Wow, what a lovely person. You certainly aren't going to be his favorite."

"No matter, as long as I'm your favorite."

"If you're too cute, I'm going to miss you more," I laughed. "I should go, but tell our cat baby I'm excited to meet them."

"Will do. You sure you don't want me to pick you up at the airport?"

"It's a waste of money since you'd basically just be sharing a cab with me."

"So?"

"Don't worry about it. I really gotta go now. Love you." I swore there was a sigh before he said it back.

Even though Scott wasn't here in London, I could still hear an old comment on how it really didn't rain *that* often. Brought up once and now forever cataloged in my head, like any other bit of information. When I got bored waiting for my ride to the airport, I looked up how right he was.

I pulled up the collar of my jacket against the brewing storm. Statistics didn't do me any good now that I was caught in a storm. I don't have any idea how others managed to sort these thoughts, all organized so illogically. It was far from the order that UltSyn promised. Security measures when traveling felt equally as unorganized, but it wasn't my detail's fault. More the nature of having one in the first place. I didn't feel free again until I was back in Japan.

After landing, the line for taxis here also looked full. I could follow a group headed for the rail, or try around the corner where one might be waiting outside a hotel. I pulled my jacket tighter, determined to do just that, as one pulled up.

Grinning at my luck, I opened the door and gave the driver the address. The driver's eyes shifted in the rearview mirror from me to the seat over in the back.

I nearly jumped when I found Scott sitting there. "Shit, I didn't see you. What are you doing here?"

"I missed you, too."

Scott raised an eyebrow at the silence that followed. He lost the staring contest, and looked away. "Well, you heard the lady," he said to the driver before turning back to me. "I wanted to surprise you. Maybe take you out for dinner, or volunteer to make you something at home. Where are we going?"

"We?"

We, Scott, signed, without looking my way. His chest had puffed up, annoyed, but clearly not trying to direct it at me. This was a nice gesture, but I had wanted some alone time after being watched for days. When I wasn't making a public statement, there was still speculation over where I was. At best, I was surrounded by security that pretended not to have eyes on me.

"I was going to get sushi by myself."

He rolled his eyes, again not directly at me however. "Just, stop the car."

"Keep driving. We'll go."

"Yamete kudasai," Scott said to my surprise. The cabbie once again looked between us, unsure what to do. A fight in the back of his cab is the last thing he wanted, and he pulled over.

"Your Japanese has gotten better since I left." My eyes fell to the door handle on his side, untouched for now.

"Almost like it's been forever," he said snidely, and knew it. "I'm sorry. You can have your night to yourself, I just wish you had told me instead of making it all about how picking you up was inconveniencing me."

Now his hand reached for the door. "Please stay," I said to the driver as I followed Scott out the same side.

I caught his hand and he pulled back away but didn't take another step.

"What?"

"Lately everything's been so planned," I said, "even this sushi night which was meant to be spontaneous. I should have embraced the magic that is you." He didn't seem convinced, so I went on. "Please come have sushi with me."

Scott bit his bottom lip, which might have looked like a suggestion on someone else. Most body language interpretation was meant for the majority. The minority is often considered too small of a factor. A percent deemed not important enough. Just like the weather, everything changes when you live it.

Not seeing this was a habit from an old system I wanted to change.

"Okay. I'm sorry," Scott said, soft enough to be a whisper, a prayer. "I love you and I keep feeling your project has been taking that."

I tried to think of something to say that would prove that false. I blinked up at the dark sky, and a raindrop hit my nose. "It was also raining in London."

"And?"

I was smiling when I looked back. "Some things remain true across borders. I love you, too, and nothing is going to change that fact."

"Come on." There was a tiredness in his steps that hadn't been there moments before as he opened the cab door for me.

It started raining harder once we were inside the cab again. Scott took an extra second, tilting his head up towards the clouds. I felt as if we'd narrowly avoided multiple things just now. "Same address as before?" Scott asked.

After a nod from me the driver put the car back in gear. I hoped we hadn't been the strangest pair he had picked up today. Dinner was playful, but the friction started once I was home again, since Junia treated me like a stranger. Which made sense, but still hurt. I had also lost my tea room, unless I wanted to kick Casio out.

I had resorted to trying to bribe the cat with leftovers when I was suddenly and forcefully made to remember how thin some Japanese walls are. From my spot on the floor trying to convince the cat out of the closet, I heard the boys in the other room.

"You know how Ada became interwoven with the system she was put on?" Scott asked.

"Yeah?"

"Do you think that could happen to a person? That connecting directly with an AI whose sole purpose is to remain in existence could change someone's decision?"

"Uhh, shit. I don't know."

Junia meowed as if adding to the conversation before hopping off a shelf and running past. I stayed put, hoping to hear more of the conversation, but they either were speaking more softly or had stopped completely.

I reached my hand up on a higher shelf to help pull myself up. My fingers brushed against something cool, and when I stood up fully, I touched a gun. When Scott stepped into the room there was a whole different topic I wanted to discuss. "What's this?"

"What's what?"

I grabbed the gun and held it out. *"This."*

"It's an airsoft pistol," Scott said, as I just continued to stare. "Casio gave it to me after someone broke into his place."

"You shouldn't have it."

Scott tilted his head as if he suddenly didn't follow. "I agree. I couldn't think of a good way to get rid of it since people sometimes check our trash. Why are you so upset tonight?"

I held back, opting to change the subject as I put the airsoft back down. "Why didn't you tell me Casio was staying here," I said quietly.

"I... thought I did?"

"No, I mean, it's like I came back to an extra roommate and a cat."

Scott laughed as he made a skewed expression. "Both just sort of happened. Maybe I undersold them because I didn't want you to feel like you were being replaced, when I really needed the company."

The house shook and I swore the night would end with an earthquake. The flashes outside the window suggested a thunderstorm instead. It was loud and overbearing and nothing I wanted to be right now. "It's just been a hell of a day. Can we start this whole night over and cuddle down while listening to the rain?"

"You've become a softie," Scott smiled softly. "I like it."

"Maybe we've both gone soft."

"Probably. With our house, an adopted cat, and a live-in hacker."

I couldn't help but laugh on my way to get pajamas out of my bag. I had brought my favorite set along, but nothing compared to the comfort of your own bed. "None of those three promised cuddles."

<chapter twenty-four>
<! -- Scott -->

In the morning, Sonia was bouncing up and down on the bed like it was Christmas. I tried to just ignore her, at very least until she upped her game and brought coffee, but it was getting ridiculous. "*St-ah-p*, okay, you win. What?"

"You said you didn't understand what I did, so now that I'm back I can show you firsthand."

I sat up a little. "You planned a meeting for the day after you came back?"

"In my defense, the festival happens every year."

"Still don't follow."

Sonia grabbed one of our pillows and swung it like the holiday had turned into a pillow fight. "Be able to embrace a happy change. Isn't that exactly what you were giving me shit for in the taxi?"

"Sorry, sorry, could you at least give me some idea what festival it is?"

"It's the Osaka Mecha Happy Festival," Sonia said, which sounded both fun and fake. "The event itself is free but it's 300 yen to enter Osaka Castle."

"Okay, why not."

We took the Osaka Loop Line to a verifiable castle in the sky. Upon raised platforms that had to be 30 feet of cut rock tall was a five-story castle. Each floor was slightly smaller than the one below, allowing for a matching set of green and gold roof trimming.

"There's a total of 15 acres," Sonia said. "Originally used from 1583 to 1868, and today hosting a costumed dance contest."

I whistled at the scale of the building. To think it had been standing in this exact spot for centuries.

"Do you want to see something that might be considered morbid before we do the more kid stuff?"

"Uh, maybe? I don't know how this is related to your work."

"We are waiting for someone, now hush, and travel with your own personal tour guide." She led me around, sometimes moving with the flow of people, sometimes trying to cross their path without being overly disruptive. Sonia stopped at a stone tombstone that sat in a garden. Flowers and maybe even a small shrine were set up in front. "A mother and son, once the most powerful in Japan, committed suicide here after losing control of the castle."

The context left me speechless. Standing didn't feel like enough, so I glanced around and copied what others were doing and put my hands flat together as if with prayer. I was almost haunted with not knowing if they were heroes or villains of their time.

"They were so upset with the end of their legacy," Sonia continued, "but here it is still."

"Here it is," I repeated, but had doubts. This place was beautiful, but how much did this type of immorality cost them who they really were, what they actually felt and believed in. Maybe if I looked on long enough, I'd figure it out.

"Oh shoot, it took us longer to get here than I thought." She was looking down at her phone before texting something. "Least I know where William and his family are now so I can introduce you."

"What did they do?"

"He works with me and Elliot?"

"No, I know that." My focused stayed on the grave marker. "What did *this* family do?"

"Unify Japan."

I nodded weakly, and followed Sonia to wherever we were meant to meet up, all while wishing that unity wasn't one of those positive-sounding words that could be far too easily misused.

William was easy to spot, even before we reached him. Something about how he held himself made him the only likely option. He was outside the castle while a kid next to him was tugging on his mother's arm to go in.

"Sonia, it's been too long," William joked, and I did my best not to cringe, since they were just in London together. Maybe not even twenty-four hours ago.

"For sure," Sonia bantered back. "Scott, this is William, and his wife Eiko-san, and their son."

"Nice to meet you," I said, and turned enough to bow towards his wife.

She returned the gesture quickly before whispering to her son. "Excuse us," she said before taking her son to where he was insisting.

William chuckled nervously as if she were being offensive, which she hadn't been. "He's performing today and wanted to meet up with his friends first. After the show, I'd be happy to show Scott the building."

"Perfect," Sonia said before I could ask what building.

We found our seats, or rather William guided us to where he said our seats were. It was near the front, and I felt like we had come far too late to deserve this spot. To be honest, William struck me as the sort that wouldn't even stick around to watch.

He stayed, and I didn't mind being wrong on that front. The music changed and a group of small children, dressed in the same red and black I'd seen her son in, came out on stage. No wonder his son had been so pushy about getting ready. There'd been so little time.

Their dance was bouncy, and felt modern but I could have been completely off-base. The routine lasted a few minutes before they snapped into a new pose and met with a polite chorus of chapping. The next routine looked more like a martial art.

As the kids filed off stage, William suggested we head over. Again, the where was excluded, but I decided to just watch, since doing so was telling me more about him than words were. We walked past the castle grounds to an office building that looked state-of-the-art in comparison.

The front room looked like it had been cut in half. It was an odd rectangle of space, both too wide and too short at the same time. I realized how right I was until Sonia entered a code on a machine that looked as boring as it possibly could have.

A wall slid back and over to reveal a new path. Off from what would've been the rest of the office was a set of metal stairs lit by a red light that shined from two flights down.

William held a card over a wide metal door with a large window set into it. By the type, I bet it was even bulletproof. Behind it was another, and a pentagon-shaped room after both. I almost had missed the few servers in the room, since a window overlooked the largest server farm I had ever seen.

Sonia's voice carried up from behind me. "UltSyn's problem was that it traded in secrets. But, all of this information was freely given. Needs and wants posted constantly but had no system to categorize or fulfill them. We plan to organize that."

Speechless, that's what I was. This was a beyond-revolutionary idea.

"It will show people that the world doesn't operate on capitalism, or even money. It runs off systems like these," William said, stepping into view with his arms up. "What do you think?"

"I think you could change the world."

Sonia's eyes lit up, wide enough to catch all the stray lights from the machines. "Really? You believe in this idea? Or at least understand why I've been retooling them to hold only what has been publicly offered?"

"It's the most game-changing idea I ever heard." At my words, William smiled and relaxed to lean against a sliver of wall next to the glass. A high voltage box nested above his head with yellow and red cords twisting up and through the ceiling.

<chapter twenty-five>
<! -- Scott -->

It was an odd feeling to hate things you knew you once might have liked. On my way back from the corner store, a sign overhead caught my eye. The background looked like a blue skyscape with so few details, it likely blended in at just the right time of day to make the large hand to the right look like it was floating. Quite literally hovering in the masculine hand was a cellphone that reached past the sign's border. The screen asked a question: *Are you safe?*

"Fear-mongering douchebags." I wondered if I could get up there, but promised myself I'd think out a full plan before I made an attempt.

At least there was one perk of having more roommates than originally planned. Because we had a tiny kitchen, Casio offered to take over the dishes, promising to put them away for me if given first crack at making food. Since that would finish off my to-do list, I agreed and opened my laptop.

"I never should've named this program after a real person. The code is still messed up after our patch and I feel like I'm letting the real Lovelace down," I complained sometime later as Casio brought me a dinner bowl.

"The real person was from the early eighteen hundreds, she'd find all of this beyond impressive. I get what you mean though. What's wrong with it?

"It's just not… behaving how it should."

"Hmm, well eat and maybe you'll figure it out."

"Yes, mother."

Casio faked a gasp. "What happened to *honey?*"

"Shut up," I laughed. It would have been embarrassing to admit just how much better my chest felt for the crack in tension. "If you give me any more shit, I'm only going to ask Sonia for help from now on."

"Fair, but I can't help you anyways. I am working on a print that can ruin flash photography to help protect the identity of protesters."

"That's really smart, do you need help?"

"Nope, but I'll bring you in if I get stuck."

I finished eating, but still hadn't made a breakthrough. When Sonia walked by, I reached for her hand. "My baby, my love, come here."

She took a few steps over so she could actually reach my hand. "Hi." She smiled even after she came around to see what was on the screen. "What do you want?"

"Want to go on a short adventure with me?"

"Alright, what sort?"

"Just going for a walk to see if Ada is working correctly."

Sonia shrugged a shoulder then grabbed her jacket. "Can we play with the profiler?"

"Don't call it that," I laughed. "It makes me feel like a cop."

"Then what would you call it?"

"A bit of programming that checks location data against time stamps to tell what is going on around you," I said. Sonia pursed her lips together and just waited. "Fine. It's a profiler until I can think of something less wordy."

"There you go."

We walked to a cafe, ordered, and sat down on the same side of the table. It felt overly cute, even though I only did it so Sonia could easily see the tablet with me. I pulled up a heat map of changes made to an online database. Dots of color appeared and showed the country of origin up. If I clicked on any one, it told me what the edit was.

It was defaulted to check for English, so I changed it over to Japanese. Reading the characters was tricky, so Sonia translated. "Keiji Muto, believe that's a professional wrestler." Someone in Japan adding a note about a Japanese celebrity made sense.

"This one?" I clicked on a dot coming from China.

"Uh, Military Academy." She leaned in since the symbols were small. "List of alumni."

"Little weird." I narrowed the search down to people in Japan, and then down to people in our ward. No results popped up, and I wondered if the whole system was lagging. But slowly a few finally populated. The only edit made in the area was to something called Stigmata of the Wind. "Okay, that's much weirder than the last thing."

Sonia leaned close as if checking the spelling before looking it up on her phone. "It's a light novel series. Left incomplete after the death of the author."

"And now I'm sad. Let's test a more local approach."

I glanced around, looking for something acceptable to point Ada at when Sonia dropped her scone to quickly have her hands free. "Let me."

She held her hand out and I offered out the tablet. It wasn't huge, but when she held it up as if to take a photo of the two people in the corner, I thought I'd die of embarrassment. Both were hanging out together, but on their phones. At least they didn't seem to notice.

An image slowly appeared, coming into focus like a developing polaroid. "Posted about their drinks," Sonia said, with a pleased smile. She glanced up from the screen to the two people. "I wonder which one of them it belongs to."

"It's lagging." I was far less impressed. "Hallie could have done it faster."

"Wasn't Hallie hooked into more powerful systems? Can't blame your re-work for the delay."

"Guess so." I reached over to steal a bite of Sonia's scone. Sharing hadn't been the plan, but an objection would be better than this topic. While more machines could mean more horsepower, it also could mean more noise to sort through. Searching for anything and everything streaming into the void wasn't how you went anywhere fast. Ada was designed to work like the tip of an arrow. Quick and targeted.

"Can't solve every mystery, love," Sonia said, and I realized just how well she could still read me.

***

Discouraged by several minor annoyances, one literally still looming, I decided to do something about it. Our kitchen was free, so I measured out a 1:4 ratio of wheat flour to water before dumping the water in a pot to boil. Once bubbles started to appear, I poured the flour in and stirred to avoid getting any clumps. After it was all nice and glue-like, I poured it into a to-go container. The image I wanted was easy to find since it was covered under Unicode, so once printed, the only thing else I needed was scissors and a paintbrush.

Getting to the roof of the apartment building I saw the billboard before was actually pretty easy, since the previous visitors had left the door deliberately ajar. The city beyond looked dusty, and I walked to the corner edge of the building, having one foot on each side where the roof met at a point. I expected the city below to look small, but the view only reminded me how large it was. Brimming with more people, buildings, and history shrouded within each other.

A chain-link fence divided the roof, and through it was the back of the sign I wanted to tag. I stepped back and walked over. With one foot, I jumped to give myself enough height to grab the top bar, and pulled myself over. This side had graffiti, but since it wasn't in view it had been left alone long enough that the colors had been baked by the sun. Broken-down cardboard boxes were laid out by the side, occasionally marked with excess paint. The billboard had a comically small step ladder with only two steps welded to the frame.

Are you safe? The question hung over my thoughts of where I wanted to place my poster. I dragged over a cinder block for a boost. I painted the wheat paste over the fake screen, before carefully lifting the pink sakura flower I'd printed up. The urge to re-stick it a dozen different ways was tempting, but I had made a choice and literally had to stick with it. I shook a can of spray paint, and enjoyed the rattle. Next to the old manipulative message, I scrawled *#WeGotThis.*

I got down, backing up as far as I could to get a better look. The combination of spray paint and paper worked well with the dystopian image struggling to peek through the blossom. With a smile, Seiji's words came to me. "If it is hidden, it is a flower."

The sky darkened only moments before the clouds started to drizzle. I lifted my face to the rain and ended up sitting down with my feet hanging off the roof. I couldn't see my house with the taller buildings in the way, but a tucked-away cell tower served as a marker, and a reminder.

I had been working off the idea that Ada was slowing down because there were extra copies out in the world. But a call made from home to someone else in the house would *first* reach out to that tower...

<chapter twenty-six>
<! -- Sonia -->

"But Russia? Sonia, Russia?"

It was nearing illogical how many times we'd had this debate. Maybe if the topic hadn't been hijacked by fear of losing what we already had, this loop could have been fixed. But then again, without it, maybe the conversation would have broken down entirely. "It will be fine, it's a safer country now."

"Their definition of safety is what worries me."

"Should location dictate who we help?" I knew I had him there and his expression confirmed it. "You said you were fine with me doing this. If it makes you feel better, I do have my own security."

"You'd better call me. *Daily.* I don't care what time it is," he said, and I wondered if anything could ease his worry instead. "I always miss you when you leave. Just… everything feels off without you around."

"Don't try to charm your way into getting me to stay; you know I wouldn't go unless I absolutely believed this was the right thing." I leaned in and his lips quaked against mine. The hands cradling my face almost pulled me up to my tiptoes. It was a kiss that restlessly demanded not to be the last. For everything it was, it was still a kiss on my way out of the door.

* * *

Russia had plenty to see, centuries of its own history. One look at Saint Basil's Cathedral and you knew that, but business trips left no time to explore. My usual security detail traveled with me, but having a driver this time felt like reaching a whole new level.

While working, Michael and Elliot wore solid black trimmed with thin armor. I thought their helmets would grow tiresome, especially after socializing more casually, but if anything I liked them more now. I enjoyed being seen as the authority to speak wherever we went. Recognizable, while they were faceless details.

We went straight to the hotel, a suite that felt as large as the house in Japan. I scanned the room-service menu as my bags were brought in. When food arrived, they silently ate dinner in the corner to preserve some personal space. Well, if you could call meal-replacement drinks dinner. Oh, how the tables had turned so much. This was a future I had never imagined.

I returned my plate to the room service cart so it could be rolled out, and caught Elliot reaching towards a chess set on an end table. It had been my one special request when booking. Pieces on both sides of the board were white. Elliot's finger twitched, holding himself a hair's width away from a knight.

"If you move the pieces on me, I won't be able to remember whose piece is whose." At my voice he fell into attention as a guard, and not a person. It was his job, but I still frowned. "It's a replica of Yoko Ono's board. Do you know what she said about it?"

Elliot shook his head, so slight that only the lights reflecting on his helmet showed the tiny change.

"You play by trust, until you can't remember which pieces are your opponent's and which pieces are yours."

If he was interested, he made no further sign of it. No suggestion that he wanted to play, no tilt of the head over the idea, nothing. It's a shame Scott couldn't come to Russia. He would have been fascinated by it.

The next morning, when I went to the hospital, it was such a casual and stress-free event that I was taken aback that there were others who regularly came to hospitals without a hint of worry plaguing them.

"I'm here to see your Chief of Medicine," I said in Russian, since everyone here would be able to understand.

"You must be Ms. Gris?"

I smiled at the name since it was both mine and not mine. The perfect thing to get me in a friendly mood and often the very thing that helped focus the attention of those who didn't take meeting with us seriously. "That's me."

"She's waiting for you." The nurse eyed the men behind me, but didn't comment before he informed us of where her office was. Down the hall and to the right. Easy.

I opened the door and the Chief of Medicine gestured for us to sit across from her. There were two chairs, and I gestured for the boys to sit as I stayed standing. The power move did not go unnoticed since she had to look up at me. "I must say I don't think I fully understood your request. The recent one that is. I know the ToS on our older equipment was recently updated."

"I need your MRI machine."

She waited for me to go on, but I didn't volunteer any details. "If you need medical help this isn't the path for that. Our contact says you can't remove the machine from the building." Her hand moved to sit on the pile of paperwork that I assumed were the very contacts.

"That's true," I said, folding my hands behind me. "About the machine, but the software it runs off can be updated or even pulled at any time."

The accusation seemed to change the temperature in the room. "Are you holding my hospital ransom?"

"Even before I took over, UltSyn had issued a mandatory recall and refusing to allow me access to it technically holds *my* assets under ransom." I walked the length of her desk before looking back over at her. "Now I wouldn't want to force your hospital to buy all-new, leaving your patients without in the meanwhile. Simply fulfill my request and I'll be happy to let you all get back to business."

She crossed her legs, sitting up taller, then just as quickly uncrossed them. "Fine, but I expect no further delays for my doctors."

"Thank you." I said with a smile as Elliot got up to open the door for me.

"I'd be careful," she added to Michael, who hadn't stood yet. "When people look down on you, they aren't exactly charitable about it." I wasn't even sure if he knew Russian. Language skills were a department I didn't need him to cover.

The MRI was located in a different building, but this time I didn't need a guide to find it. I stared at the large machine, finding it interesting despite its age. Similar tech like transcranial electromagnetic scanners could even turn parts of the brain on and off. UltSyn had gotten all the way to optogenetics, but that field was far less commercial than classic diagnostic equipment.

Through the glass booth Elliot signed, *Ready.*

I ventured over to the workstation he was at. The system's weak point wasn't the connection, or the age of the equipment—it was the UltSyn code. A backdoor that led straight to the heart of everything that used the same legacy AI that I had been connected to. What was once their control collar was now my ring of keys. We lifted what amounted to access codes before restarting the machine. Delaying a few tests was such a small cost in the grand scale of things. "Time to storm the castle, boys."

Even with targeting the closest hospital that was exploitable, it was a two-hour drive to where we needed to go next, this time taking full control of the radio until we'd parked around the side. The car was hidden behind some trees, since being the only one might raise suspicion.

The building was a design wonder of its own, but UltSyn's finest would soon be remade in my image. The image of all those harmed behind its walls. And the prize was won with a final touch. I hit a button on my phone and it sent a signal to every connected system inside. From heating to lighting, all came to life again with my patch update.

I stood just inside the entrance until every last light twinkled back on. Without a big bang, a whole new universe was created. Inside was silent for everything except the subtle buzz of tech and distant insects.

Signage showed what floors had marketing, R&A, and several other things that had their letters knocked to the floor—probably from the time of UltSyn's crash, considering the dust. Much of this building was wasted space, dressed up as forward-thinking; the things excluded from the list said more.

We headed to an unlisted underground level that was designed to stay cooler. It looked worse than I had expected. Like a bomb shelter that had been looted rather than declared a sanctuary. Metal plates on the ground had been lifted; I carefully leaned over into the manhole created around the large pipes below. They appeared fine, but would've been impossible to move and made of a common metal. Gold and copper plating, and other things that were easily stolen, had already been taken.

The thought held no water, but I almost expected to see someone down there to match the Russian saying, *We thought we had hit rock bottom, and then someone knocked from below.* Everything left was fixed in place or without value, like a knocked-over water cooler. I touched an empty bottle with my shoe and it rolled further down the ramp. The MRI had jump-started the system, allowing me to power things back on so the ambience shouldn't matter.

Japan's buildings had been well-preserved, leaving hope that the damage was reserved to more public areas. In a shared office, I found a smashed security camera. Maybe near the end, someone thought UltSyn would come back and charge them for property damage.

We walked on until we reached a control room, the only room that held a similar vibe to Japan's building. On a monitor overlooking everything was a DOS-looking screen full of text, with a window that read *System Rebooted.* I clicked okay and the text scrolled up with a real-time readout.

There was a familiar and uncomfortable feeling in my spine.

"Step away," Michael ordered with a gun pressed to my back. I suddenly hated the sound of his voice, but the feeling of being shot point-blank had never been appealing.

I brought my hands up and started to slowly turn. He gave me just enough room to follow his instructions. "Go ahead, Elliot."

He nodded curtly, then moved to where I was standing. It was only a few keystrokes before he hit a very loud snag. The lights shifted into low power mode as an alarm blared from speakers that had seen better days since their installations.

"What's wrong?" Michael asked. Elliot shook his head and continued typing. Annoyed and with nothing to do, Michael gestured over to the corner with a gun. "Stand there."

That was further away from anything useful, but I didn't see any other option. He didn't move, just kept his eyes and gun trained.

The alarm stopped and Elliot turned away from the console. He stepped towards Michael, grabbing his wrist, and twisted so the gun would fall. The cry that followed seemed like a finger got broken.

With the gun securely in Elliot's hands now, I took a step towards Michael. "Tell me why I shouldn't have him shoot you."

No answer.

"Fine, shoot him."

Hesitation predated the shoot. The gun lowered from Michael's chest to his knee. This time the scream didn't even sound like his voice. Michael crumbled to the ground while Elliot's chest heaved before pulling out the clip and tossing the pieces separate directions. The helmet came off next, and any thanks I would have given was stolen from my lungs. Standing where Elliot *should have been* was Scott.

"Take off your helmet," I yelled to Michael.

His hands were pressed against the hole in his leg. "Now?" he gritted out.

"Do it!"

The blood on Michael's hands smeared on the clean helmet as he pulled it off. Beside a sheet of sweat, it was still him. *We had been friends.* "Stay silent and maybe you'll see your family again."

With a roll of his eyes, Michael went back to trying to avoid too much blood loss. *One turncoat, and one stolen identity.*

"You followed me here?" My question to Scott sounded unsure, despite the very obvious answer.

"No, love." Scott reached an arm out, and pointed to the machines. "I followed her."

I glanced over, not following the her in question. It was a collection of machines; they weren't personified or even an OS that spoke. "Ada," I said as it dawned on me. I had integrated Scott's code to power my own, and he finally tracked down the reason it was lagging. *Me.*

"I risked everything I had," he started, "everything I now am to come here. And we should go now."

I shook my head. "You came because Ada told you I was in danger?"

"If she could read the intentions behind a mask, neither of us would be here," he said, although somehow not unkindly.

"Then why?"

"The 'good family man' moved against you first, but it was only a matter of time. Systems like this cannot exist in the hands of the few. This is the last link of your new system, and since you added my code everywhere, it was easy to spoof what I needed." I opened my mouth to ask another question, but he held up a finger. "It's my turn to ask a question. I didn't come because I'm worried about you, because I believe even if you are lost, you can find your way."

"Then why are you here?" I interrupted. "Are you suggesting it gets better? Being lost?"

"It gets different," Scott said, "and can get better."

There was a man bleeding in the same room as us—I could hardly picture us having this conversation even without that glaring detail. "None of that is a question."

"No, it wasn't." His tone somehow held the same uncertainty he had before when kissing me. "Things we create should be for us. My question is, in this new world where secrets and wants are gone, what do people do?"

"What? Why would they have to do anything?"

He smiled and it quickly spread over his tight expression. The irony of me saying that when he had been the first to do so with the day laborers was not lost. "Day to day," he continued, "in this perfect system, how do people fill their time? Are they happy? Do they have fun?"

I looked down, wanting to check my work, but ended up looking at my shoes. A glance at all my work wouldn't hold the answer either. "Yes, of course."

"You might be following the law, but haven't considered the ethics. The moment you do something with the freely given information, it's no longer just data. It's forced to follow the rules of the algorithm you wrote. If a person mentions a want, and you search for a match to that request, where is the choice? People don't naturally act on every thought they have."

There was a heaviness in my stomach. "And you'd suggest what?"

"This plan marries you to UltSyn. Part of its past, present, and future. I can't see you wanting that, so why are you denying yourself what you want to give others? You still can find peace where you can. That's not failure."

I felt my eyes start to water, like a tidal wave of heartbreak over something long ago.

Scott took my hand and went on. "The act of your continued existence ensures the story never fades. UltSyn lives, but do you?"

<! -- Scott -->

I didn't really believe what had happened. If it even really was only last night since the mental divide felt like an eternity. I pushed myself up from the bed, blinking hard against the morning light. In large part, I was still in armored gear from before. The room held the neutrality of a hotel room, but a single glance out the window showed smoke from chimneys in the distance and brick buildings accented with red. *Still in Russia.*

I let the drapes fall away from my fingers and stared at the empty bed. For all my plans, weapons, and tech, it had come down to pleading. The sound of the gunshot echoed in my head and I winced at the sound. A nagging reminder that I'd done something I'd promised myself I wouldn't do again. *God, I should have planned past this point.*

We had left Michael there, not to die, but to plan his own rescue. Whether that was the cops or if someone else in on his plan came to help, I didn't know. Our ignorance could be more dangerous than leaving a weapon.

A mechanical lock turned across the room and the door opened. *Anyone unfriendly meant*— Before I could finish the thought, Sonia's shape filled the void and I wished I was more relieved than I felt. I had convinced her against pursuing the massive privacy violation that was designed to help, but I don't think either of us were too sure of our choices.

I mean, I knew UltSyn was *bad* and a government-less Big-Brother style system built from a corporation's corpse would also be bad. But I couldn't help but feel like I had also pleaded against the good she was also trying to bring. If one could buy into the 'ends justify the means' mentality, that is, and I didn't know if I did anymore.

My silent staring was met with its own lack of eye contact. Sonia stopped in front of me, lifting up a cardboard carrier that held two to-go cups of coffee. I was at a loss for words when I took the closest one. Maybe we'd both spoken our piece last night and there wasn't even a syllable left to spare.

Sonia sat on the end of the bed, staring at the black screen of the TV for a moment before taking a sip of coffee. It was too hot, but her control didn't let more than a twitch through. "I don't have a plan to get you home."

Us home, I thought, but the correction was born from desperation and need. After mentally kicking myself, the intent was clear. She had specifically meant me. Her flight back would be perfectly legal. I was the one with a visa that said it couldn't leave Japan. We could try, but we'd have to explain ourselves and hope they'd be cool with my ignoring the rules. Both ways.

"Me, either." I took a sip of coffee absentmindedly, and expected it to burn my tongue, but it wasn't hot after all. Maybe I had misread her.

Still, the reminder that I wasn't meant to be here grew until I had to move again, this time opting to sit in the chair next to the window. Which brought little comfort, but with the pulled curtains it would have to be good enough for now.

"What was your plan if I hadn't shown up?"

Sonia finally met my gaze. Maybe also misreading me for a moment. "Continue working on the system. Likely here in Russia for a while."

"You still haven't really befriended Junia."

The question of why that was important seemed to show on her face. But it was... everything. A whole chain of possibilities that would have been lost by her not coming home. The person she was, the people we could become, altered forever by that one variable. Could I live with someone who casually forced a wild change without even allowing them a clear opt-in or opt-out? What was the saying I hated back in the U.S.? That type of freedom wasn't free.

Sonia got up, took the step needed to reach me, and placed a hand on my arm. "You're shaking, are you okay?"

I closed my eyes, trying to get a hold of myself. My thoughts screamed that they wanted to be at home, rather than jail. Or in this country, where it was legal to ship me back to London for just that— a possibility I had been once ready for, after taking on UltSyn. But that all changed after Sonia. Even where home now was turned out to be far different than I ever would have guessed. I wanted to go back to Japan more than run out the clock of my old life, because that was a series of variables that no longer had any power to them.

"I'm fine, I just need to get somewhere safe." Our tones were far too serious, but at least we had words. "I doubt I'd be allowed to stay here, even if I wanted, unless I became a symbolic tool. What do you want?"

"Sunlight," she said, eyes glancing up to the window, her hand rubbing my arm as she went on. "Honestly."

I smiled, almost laughed thinking back. "With your comrades?"

She nodded, and I shook my head a little. This possibility could have been too easily lost, and that was a sobering fact.

"You know I wouldn't have stopped you if I thought it would have gained you those things."

Sonia placed her drink down and sat down on the near edge of the bed. I curiously watched before mirroring her. "I know," she said, giving my leg a squeeze. "That's why we are partners. I love you. I hope you feel that, because it's always been enough for me to..." Sonia's words petered out, before her gaze met mine. "Hold on to, even if it's actually also something for myself."

I nodded along as she finished. "By loving others, we learn to love ourselves. When done flawlessly it creates a cycle of care. Imperfection might be how this all started, but love is still the spark that powers all the positive change in the world. So, I say, here's to us." I grabbed my drink for a toast. "And to our great escape."

End of Line

Author Acknowledgements

This book is an act of self-love that almost did not get made in a million different ways. We'd like to thank our editor, Doctor O'Mara for keeping the dream alive. There's no better person to end an era with, thank you so much for providing the final piece with your actions.

To each other, it's been a rocky road and being able to still have this story and have love between us is something beautiful.

To any reader who was here since our debut, or recently found us, thank you so much. Words cannot do justice for the feeling of being able to share these characters with you.

About The Authors

Rose Sinclair is the profane community leader that started Fuck Yeah Asexual in 2013. The biggest noise maker they spearheaded was the #GiveItBack protest in 2015 that made GLADD step up for asexual, aromantic, and agender people, paving the way for future acceptance of those communities and on-screen representation. They popularized several community terms and built a decentralized support system with a "Dear Abby" style approach. They are the author of HELLO WORLD, leader of community projects such as WHAT YOU SEE, with more novels to come.

Loving cat mom and wife, Alexandra Tauber grew up with a strong love for science fiction, comic books, and games. A growing love for storytelling helped formed her aspirations to write novels, driving her at an early age to practice writing in online roleplay forums. Alex plans to work on and develop diverse, compelling narrative driven video games as another exploration for her love of storytelling. Most days, Alex spends her free time cuddling her cat, cooking a bomb ass meal, or playing a whole lot of video games.

Thank you so much for reading Scott and Sonia's story. If you've enjoyed *Variable Current* please consider leaving a review on Amazon and check out other books by us.

www.ingramcontent.com/pod-product-compliance
Lightning Source LLC
Chambersburg PA
CBHW022157260626
47155CB00019B/3065